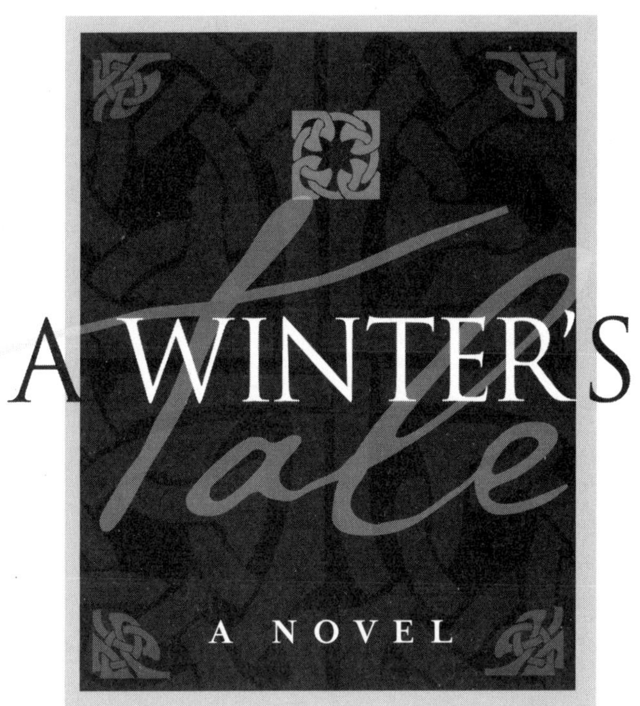

A WINTER'S tale

A NOVEL

GAIL SIDONIE
SOBAT

Second Printing, 2005

Great Plains Publications
420 – 70 Arthur Street
Winnipeg, MB R3B 1G7
www.greatplains.mb.ca

Great Plains Publications gratefully acknowledges the financial support provided for its publishing program by the Government of Canada through the Book Publishing Industry Development Program (BPIDP); the Canada Council for the Arts; as well as the Manitoba Department of Culture, Heritage and Tourism; and the Manitoba Arts Council.

Design & Typography by Relish Design Studio Ltd.
Printed in Canada by Friesens
Map drawn by Spyder Yardley Jones

CANADIAN CATALOGUING IN PUBLICATION DATA

Main entry under title:

Sobat, Gail Sidonie
A winter's tale / Gail Sidonie Sobat.

ISBN 1-894283-45-7

I. Title
PS8587.O23W55 2004 C813'.6 C2004-900394-1

For

Erin Craig Sobat
my favourite nephew

ACKNOWLEDGMENTS

Many special thanks to:
Duane Stewart, Carolyn Pogue, Mark Haroun,
Thomas Trofimuk, Merle Harris, Kathleen Evans,
Geoffrey McMaster and Jeannie Sobat.

Hinterlund
Spriggen
Spinne's domain
Brüe Wood
TO MÜLLE
Nookeshea
TO MIRT
Ruheplatz
Mountain Vale
Hören Wood
River Hören
N
W
E
S

PROLOGUE

IT IS A STARLESS NIGHT. A thick night. The air is heavy with the threat of late autumn rain. An unease has settled in the wood. Nocturnal animals scamper through the dark, as they always do and must, but they frequently pause and twitch, uncertain, too aware of a sharpness in the night. But for the occasional buzz of a pesky last insect at her sleeping ear, in the house where she dwells, there is silence. A dying fireplace ember pops the end of its glowing life. Although all else is still, her dreams are disquiet.

Leagues away in the city of Sprïggen, in the dungeon of the castle of a minor lord, a child shivers miserable in her own filth and rags. The close, humid darkness is rank with mildew, urine and vomit. A rat skitters close to the huddled form, sniffs to determine whether the morsel is worth its effort, then opts for better pickings elsewhere and slinks away through a crack in the heavy stone walls. Unaware of this or any other intruder, the small wretched form slumbers fitfully on, sob-sighing through troubled dreams.

Many miles from any city, the villagers of Mülle dance half-mad and soot-choked around a smoking fire of wet wood. Music and drums ignite the air; pockets are picked while fortunes are told. Heedless and hapless of skullduggery afoot, the villagers pound dully about, their heavy soiled boots tramping the grasses where they lurch. Near them, in the shadows, a young woman's back aches with the bow of the stock. Arms, legs, and head entrapped, she has not moved in two suns. The remains of a rotten egg stink near her left ear. When she had complained of thirst earlier that afternoon, someone had given her vinegar to drink. She hovers between waking and nightmare; they are one and the same.

And tonight, leagues away in the great city of Ruheplatz, in the light of a thousand torches, the performers of the street sweat in the toil of their crafts: balancing, juggling, knife-throwing, flame-eating, contortionism, puppetry. The din from the paying customers, their delight at the street antics, the madcap shadows of the manic acrobats serve almost to overshadow the proclamation nailed to the oak doors of the city. Almost, but not quite.

Now it is midnight. The hour of witching. Near a single barred window of the Sprïggen castle dungeon, a ginger cat pads softly, stops to lick one paw. In a flash of fiery orange, a young woman appears instead of a cat. She utters a low growling threat to the bars which bend apart at her angry will. There is now enough room for a child to escape with a quick leap and a promise.

In the same heartbeat, back in the town of Mülle, a man and a dark-haired woman break away from the lumbering stupid villagers. The swish of their silk alerts the stock-imprisoned woman that someone draws near. She wearily raises a wrecked face to gaze at the approaching tormentors.

Dazed by the flash of a gold-toothed smile, the perfume of a foreign spice, the quick click of a picked lock, she finds herself arm-swept away towards the thicket of woods where bright caravans are poised to disappear into the night.

All torches are spent now in Ruheplatz as is the money of the citizens. Coins make a satisfied clink in the deep pockets of the fire-eater. He is the last of the performers to leave the sleeping, satiated city; his band of merrymen and goodwomen have already started towards the next of the great cities. A grumbling guard, longing for surrender to his straw pallet, is eager for him to quit the gates that they might be locked. The fire-eater whistles as he ambles deliberately past the surly gatekeeper. Sets his bagatelle down on a rock and watches the closing of the doors. Heavy locks slide into place. The fire-eater takes a swig from the flask at his side and steps forward to read the proclamation in the dim cloud-covered night. He spits in revulsion at the sign, and his disgust bursts into flame. Nimble-footed, he cavorts and jigs away through the thick scrub surrounding the city. Behind him the guard roars in anger and sounds the fire alarum.

At this cadence, the bundled form turns over in her small cot to begin better dreams. Raindrops patter against her thatched roof; the forest breathes a sigh of relief. And Hana of Hören Wood gives a soft satisfied chuckle.

CHAPTER

THE CHILD SLEPT. The witch did not.

By the moonbeams of the Huntress, she could still discern no visible flaw. A tousled mass of dark curls, none reddish, as were her own. The face, soft in repose, bore no blemish or freckle. The limbs she'd bathed of grime and filth were sturdy. Two brown eyes. To all appearances, a healthy child.

Then what? What was wrong?

Ingamald observed the curled fingers, relaxed by the dreams of the dreamer. Counted and smiled. Six on one hand. The left, the sinister. Six on the other. So fixed was her witch's eye on finding some hideous deformity, Ingamald, intent on curing the child's fever, had for seven days and nights overlooked this subtlest of differences. Twelve fingers. Of course. That was the problem, the error in nature, of which they had been so afraid.

Lately, they were always afraid.

She was used to a fearful people and their ignorance. Hadn't Ingamald herself been driven from her adoptive parents, then her childhood home of Hören Wood and Hana's safe hearth by fear and ignorance? Hadn't she been friendless and misunderstood because of the colour of her copper hair, the glint of her emerald eyes? Wasn't her great gift, her power, source of both suspicion and envy?

In those five years, Ingamald had tried to assuage the fear. The peasants and farmers were good folk. Most were gentle and harmless. And she had done her best to befriend or at least win the trust of the nearby townfolk of Wellehørst. In working a spell of purification, she had cured the sick well in the centre of the village, and hence won the regard of a handful of citizens, the begrudging admiration of many others. Over five winters, the witch was increasingly sought after as word spread of her healing powers. Carefully, she tended to the aged, the infirm, to sick infants and children, always cautioning the parent or the spouse, son or daughter, that herbs and spells could only fend off death for so long. Come death would as it always has and will.

Sixty moons and no real ugliness or danger had yet visited the witch. Always she watched the faces of those she met. Seldom did a friendly gaze meet hers. Though they respected her arts, they could not forget the tales that she had destroyed her own mother, and that a power, formidable and freakish, waxed within their witch.

Though tongues wagged, their stories spun, friendless she was not. Ingamald smiled. She was blessed with a number of beloved friends. And, from what the nightbreeze told her, they had done well seven nights past.

Dear Hana was ever near, although her dwelling was leagues to the south. She and Ingamald communicated regularly by mutual acquaintance, spell and dream. Even the occasional letter. Though she had not embraced her these many years, Ingamald felt in her bones that soon she would. Ever Hana's pupil, Ingamald frequently shared with the old woman news of a latest spell or herbal remedy, a new-uncovered wisdom, through careful reading of the tome Hana had given her as a parting gift.

Then there was Sall, now the mother of five children, three boys in addition to Merelda and Freya, whom Ingamald had once cured of fever. Insistent that her witch-friend meet Zem Jr. and the twins, Piet and Gunter, Sall had left Zem in charge of the farm, hitched the mule to a rickety cart, and brought the entire brood to Brüe Wood to visit

Ingamald last midsummer. The witch marvelled at her intrepid friend's mettle and spent the week bewildered and delighted by the presence of so much chatter and life in Nookeshea, Ingamald's cramped but cosy cottage. She was lost when they departed, so starved had she been for female company and conversation.

Three years past, on a beautiful fall day, she had journeyed to Ruheplatz to bear witness to the joint weddings of Gretchen to Field, a rich lord, and Prince Ranðulfr to Karenina, a noblewoman from across the sea. As honoured guest and friend, seated on the dais with the huge wedding party, the witch was dazed by the glitter of the event and dizzied from the rich food and drink. That night, Gërt tucked Ingamald once more into the enormous bed in that same room where the maidservant had held an anxious bedside vigil throughout thc wretched night of her charge's spidervenom fever. This time dreams were pleasant, and after waking, Ingamald and she had exchanged news and pleasantries; Gërt taught the witch woman some clever tapestry stitches and walked with her in the groomed gardens.

That night's sky was alight with fireworks, the Ruheplatz streets rife with the odours of burning oil, the air awash with the noises of hucksters and the notes of minstrels. And sure enough, among the vagabond street entertainers, witch Ingamald found fire-eater Ingo. He delighted her and the others gathered with his incendiary antics for the better part of an hour; then he helped her sample the local brew at a popular alehouse. Eager to hear her version of the stories stealing out of Brüe Wood, garrulous Ingo listened and interrupted until the wee hours and the closing of the alehouse. His prattle and flirtation had greatly amused Ingamald, and with her invitation, he had since twice repaid her visit.

And it was precisely these visits that aroused the curiosity, and perhaps something else, of the Troubadour. Never far from her thoughts, often in mid-daydream or mid-study, his dark form and brilliant smile were always welcomed to her fancy. Thrice over the years had they seen each other. Once when Ingamald was midwife to Erabesque, the Troubadour's beautiful and headstrong sister. A second time at a midsummer feast, when the witch's twitching feet could no longer be still and must dance to the Troubadour's zentauri. She spent three days then in his company, with his music, his family, his kisses, before willing herself to depart. Then his last visit, shortly after Ingo's recent departure. With more than usual Musica determination, the Troubadour burst unexpectedly in to Nookeshea one rainswept early October evening.

"So. You are alone?"

"Aye, of course."

"I heard otherwise."

"Come in and shut the door, Troubadour. You are welcome to my home."

"Truly?"

"Truly. Always."

He met her gaze and shivered.

"Come to the fire. You are drenched and cold." She brought him a wool coverlet, and he stripped his wet clothes. These she hung to dry, felt his eyes upon her back.

"So. Who is he?" His usually musical voice sounded an unhappy note.

"A friend." Her red hair sparked in the firelight as she whirled to face him. "This is why you came? To interrogate me?" Her voice was sharp. This she regretted. Anger hovered between them.

She began anew. "His name is Ingo. He is a fire-eater. A juggler. An entertainer. A huckster. I suspect sometimes a thief and pickpocket. Not unlike yourself." She smiled.

The Troubadour ran his hand through damp hair. "Ingamald, I apologize. I thought you might be in danger. You are in danger. I know not whom to trust. I am mad with rage."

She came to him with a rag and dried his hair. Sparks from the fire punctuated the silence. He touched her hand.

"Who is he to you?"

"A friend. Troubadour. A friend."

"And I?"

"Aye, you are a friend, too." Ingamald smiled again at his frown. "Aye, that and more." And she kissed him.

In the morning, when he was dry and rested, she listened to him tell her what she knew in her skin. Something was amiss in the world. Some sourness in the wind. A stirring unease in the leafless trees. Birdsong of a sadder tune. Something in the sallow sunlight, the cruel chill in the air. Nature, her friend, had been trying to tell her a secret these many months.

Indeed, strange maladies hitherto unseen had sprung up amongst the simple folk who visited her. Their shoulders sagged more than usual; their eyes were red and sore; their malnourished muscles ached. Ingamald blamed the harsher weather and the meagre harvest.

But the Musica man in her cottage brought worse news.

"There is a malaise in the land, throughout Hinterlünd. It is a malady for which we, the Musica, hope you have a remedy." He paused, clearly pained.

"Mayhaps. Go on, Troubadour."

"We travel. We see. We use our wiles to make our living, and in so doing depend on the people. And although we are separate from them, have been kept apart from them, we know something is very wrong. The people are starving. In the country, the crops are poor and the fields wasted. So. The people move to the burghs where matters are worse. Ruheplatz, for one, is bulging at her seams, teeming with the peasants and wayfarers desperate for bread. Beggars and urchins squat underfoot and underfed. And worse, the city overflows with the vermin that fill any large centre. No longer just petty thieves and swindlers. Cutpurses and cutthroats, panderers and rogues abound. It is a dangerous, desperate place."

"When did this…how has this come to pass?"

"Trouble has been swirling in the winds for some time now. There is a man. A self-proclaimed Lord of Hinterlünd."

"What foolishness! Hinterlünd has no lord, no master. Hinterlünd is for all who dwell here. Creature and human and dwarf and people of the Rowan."

"So it should be as you say. But so it is not. No longer, Ingamald. This man-lord has wrought a change. He is covetous for power, for land, for riches. He has beguiled many."

"How so?"

"He has power. Some say the power of his magic. Others the power of his gold. Still others the power of his will. At the very least he wields fear."

"What is his name, this…this fearmonger?"

"Winter. Morton Winter." The Troubadour's words blew a frost into the cottage.

"I will know more."

"I have no doubt of that, Ingamald."

And he spent the day in telling. About the taxes imposed by this Morton Winter. His accession of lands, seizure of harvests and household goods upon failure of payment. The imposition of tithes and additional taxes on gathering wood, on gathering peat, and, most notably, on the wells of Hinterlünd.

At this the witch stiffened. "The wells?? The wells!! All wells are sacred, kept close and safe by the guardians of the waters. They belong to no one and everyone. Water is a birthright!"

The Troubadour nodded morosely and went on. The poorest of the folk fared worst. There were whispers that women were beaten for loitering, men for malingering, children put to toil if caught in the streets or wandering the country roads. Time spent from work was time deemed wasted. Even feast days were condemned as needless distraction from labour.

"Who are the beaters? The persecutors of the poor? The enforcers of this tyrant's rule? He cannot be everywhere at once! Indeed, I have never heard tell of him before."

"The princes and barons of the cities and counties."

"Surely not! These have ever been good to the people."

"Ah."

"Perhaps not to the Musica."

"No, not the Musica. And princes and barons are easily swayed."

"Not Ranðulfr, surely."

"Ah yes. Ingamald, even so."

Shocked, the witch padded about her small cottage, pausing to pick up Beezle, the black cat stretched languidly and impervious before the hearth. She stroked him thoughtfully. "What is one to do?"

"With the help of petty leaders, Morton Winter has begun a pernicious campaign, one which greatly imperils you, Ingamald. And me. So. I tell you now why it is I have come."

She faced him squarely. Beezle cat-stared likewise at the Musica.

"There is a program to drive those he deems unworthy, unwelcome from the land. Morton Winter wishes to be rid not only of the poor, but any he sees as weak vessels. And any who threaten his power. So. He also drives out of traditional hunting lands the Rowan peoples. He persecutes the Musica; some have been caught and publicly flogged for mischief. Any who are different, any who are outcast, any recluse or village idiot. Any worker of simple."

He paused and gathered breath.

"Any witch or wizard?" The witch's emerald eyes burned through him.

"Ah. So. You are a reader of minds, as well." And the Troubadour smiled for the first time, his gold tooth flashing.

"What more? Tell all."

"Morton Winter is no sage; he has no time for books and fears what lies within their pages. He would deny everyone access to knowledge, if he could. And indeed, he tries.

"Boys may study letters and sums briefly, but then must return to the fields, the mills, the market. Girls are forbidden knowledge. Every woman versed in words is witch.

"And above all, the magic arts are forbidden. The wizards have had to swear an oath that they will practise only upon command of the Imperial Winter."

Ingamald's mouth fell open. "And witches?"

"Are to be routed out. Where found, punished. If they repeat their offences, put to death. Already, several have been locked in stocks, publicly taunted. Humiliated."

The witch sank into a wicker-bottomed chair and hung her head. The Troubadour moved closer to her, spoke softly.

"There are burnings of books. The goodfolk of village and city surrender their texts. Bonfires rise high and send a stench into the night. Madness dances about the blaze as people celebrate the loss of what they know."

"And where there are burnings of books, burnings of people must follow," recited Ingamald miserably, remembering the lessons of history from the volumes she, herself, possessed.

"Ah. Yes. It is a dark time. In terror and suspicion, neighbour suspects neighbour. Especially when one is rewarded with coin for finding out a Learned or a witch. Petty jealousies and rivalries of the past give occasion to turn in innocent folk to the authorities. There is little enough to have. If one can grasp the land of his neighbour, then there will be more for himself. For a time. Until a new neighbour turns against the grasper."

The Troubadour paused. "And there is more. Women, girls, are especially vulnerable. Any mark. Any distinguishing or unusual feature. Any flaw or imperfection is cause enough to cry 'witch.'"

"Any with red hair." Ingamald shot him a rueful smile.

"Everywhere I have travelled these two month, I see women—pretty young maids, mid-aged goodwives, crook'd crones—ferreted out as workers of the Craft. And what is said and done to these women is enough to sicken."

She brought her gaze back to the present, to the face of the child with whom she sat. The child with fingers six and six whom they had tortured and imprisoned in a Sprïggen dungeon. An innocent.

And Ingamald wondered where she had been while much ado had been rallying in Hinterlünd. Staring at the stars. Conversing with woodland creature and occupant. Flying hither and yon on Broom Hildë for her own pleasure and practice. Observing the feasts of the year, the changes, solstice and equinox. Reading. Drowsing by the fire. Amusing herself with Beezle's play and her own. Dancing. Dreaming. Whiling away precious time.

For in the midst of her reveries, a darkling time had descended on the land and the people she loved. If Hana spoke true, and Hana always spoke true, then she, Ingamald, had a great destiny before her. She knew the prophecies surrounding her birth and her name. What fool was she to sit and weave a pleasant life for herself away from the world and its troubles? What had she been about? Wherefore had her mind been so self-occupied?

The witch gave her head a shake. No more sweet musing in Nookeshea away from the company of strangers. Time was nigh for action. And given the hurdles of the day, a witch had to use wile and guile to trip such a foe.

And she had done. At least it was a beginning. On the second and last evening of the Troubadour's stay, while he and Beezle slept in the cottage, Ingamald had slipped away towards the bogmarsh in the depths of Brüe Wood. The way was muddied from the rains. She slogged along for the better part of an hour through the gloom until the green vapours and the dank smell of the slough assured her she had arrived. Pulling her green cloak close to ward off the evening dampness, the wicca woman found a great stone on which to sit.

Focusing her energy, she cried, "Vapours of the marsh, I would speak with Hana of Hören Wood!"

At once the mist began a kind of swirling dance, fluid and circuitous. The whirling increased in pace and size, growing to a vortex of greenish phosphorescence until, quite as suddenly, it settled into a calm incandescent glow. From within its hovering midst, peered the aged Hana.

"Mira!" Hana called forth Ingamald's true name.

"Betsai!" Ingamald answered in kind. "I have terrible news to tell." As the younger witch repeated the tale of the Troubadour, the elderly woman seemed to shrink with the hearing.

"What will you do, Daughter?"

"Aye, indeed. What will I? I had hoped you would guide me."

The two wicca women gazed each at the other. Hana spoke. "You must put a spell of concealment around your cottage, and I mine."

"Aye. I have done. But I cannot live contented in the shadows while this menace spreads its contamination abroad."

The elder shook her head. "We of the Wicca have always been apart. Our work must needs be secret. Quietly we work our Craft. Ever on the margins."

"I will not be foolish. But neither will I be silent or invisible."

"I doubt you not, Mira."

Ingamald leapt from the stone and began to pace. "The Troubadour tells me of those who are imprisoned and persecuted. I will liberate as many such unfortunates as I can. Is there aught you can see?"

Hana closed her eyes in concentration. "A town, Mülle it is called. There a woman pilloried. And close kept in a Sprïggen dungeon, a child. A special child, methinks, or otherwise not noticed by the frostfiend."

"I must then find these out and free them. What think you?" Ingamald looked earnestly into Hana's greenish face.

"I think you are made of courageous mettle. But you cannot act alone, Daughter. Call upon your friends. Trust only those who trust you. Send me word. I await you." And Hana dissolved into the green mist.

The witch woman trudged back to Nookeshea and to the warmth of her hearth. From its reddish glowering, she selected one ember with her garden spade. This she took with her out into the clearing before her cottage. With a wild witch breath she set it alight in the night air.

"Find the Fire-eater and tell him."

In her mind's eye, she watched the floating spark travel through the darkness over hill and vale into a glade east of Ruheplatz City to a dying campfire next to the sleeping form of Ingo. There a pop of the spark roused him. To his left, a briar patch blazed but threw no heat.

Instead, it spoke in a woman's voice—one he recognized fondly—and urged, "Help thwart the frigid madman who claims to own Hinterlünd!"

"Aye! That buncosteerin' bindlestiff flux-eater: Winter!"

"Be sly. Be clever. Meddle and dash away. Then quick come to Nookeshea!"

"Say no more, witch! Ingo's yer man. I'll upset his frost-rimed applecart, I will!"

Satisfied that she had sparked Ingo into action, the young witch turned her mind toward the Troubadour. Over a simple breakfast with her Musica guest, Ingamald outlined a daring plan of rescue involving the Troubadour, his sister and herself. Brother and sister would fare forth to Mülle, she to Sprïggen. With his promise of return within a fortnight, Ingamald had watched him depart on horseback into the thickening trees of Brüe Wood.

Ingamald had turned then to her books, her magic texts. She read and fasted until it was time. Time to begin. Time, on a late autumnal night, to step forth from safety, from certainty. With cape and red hair askew, she soared off on sturdy Broom Hildë towards Sprïggen and the wretched child imprisoned therein. The child, Ingamald-turned-cat, had freed.

This child now beside her. Asleep. At peace. After a haunted week of delirium and night terrors. At last gentle repose. This child hated and reviled because of a finger extra on each hand. Who would fear something so insignificant? So harmless? So innocent? Who would fear a girlchild?

"Morton Winter," she breathed. And an icicle pierced her heart.

CHAPTER

"MORRRTTTOOOOOON!" a first voice wheezed against the latticed window.

"Cooorrrneeeliiiuuussssssss!" a second voice whispered down the fireplace chimney.

"Wiiinnnttteeer!" a third whined at the shutter.

The supine form roused and sat upright in his trapezoidal bed. Put bony white fists into his eyes to rub away the remnants of a sound, deep sleep. Untroubled by pleasant dreams. He smiled. He had done away with pleasant dreams long ago.

Adjusting his white nightcap, he swung bony white legs over the side of the great crooked white bed, thrust off the downy white covers, slipped veiny feet into silver slippers, awaiting and expectant, near the bedside.

"Good morn, Morton," sighed the left.

"Good morn, Morton," echoed the right.

"Ah yes," the man rubbed his slim pale hands together. "Ah yes!" He tossed a silver gown over the shroud of his nightshirt and stepped into the day.

"Monday. A goodish day."

He leapt to the window. Unleashed the shutters, threw open the sash. Cold, crisp air leapt in. He breathed deeply. Wheezed. Coughed.

"A perfect day!"

He shut the window and read the patterns of the frost written on the pane. "A love poem. For me. About me." He scrawled his name into the frost with his long, sharp fingernail. "And by me."

He gave a wheezy little laugh. Jigged merrily over to the silver cord near the bed and pulled it. Somewhere else a sonorous bell tolled.

Immediately, the silver door in the opposite wall opened and a host of servants, prim and white, marched neatly into the large austere room.

"Good morning, Sir," they trumpeted in unison.

One carried towels and a white basin of cold water. Another shaving implements. A third and fourth went instantly to the bed with clean white linens. A fifth attended promptly to the chamber pot. Several began polishing the silver bedstead. Three others tied open the heavy, grey velvet curtains, permitting entrance to the weak white sun. Two others coaxed and lit the fire in the great greystone fireplace. Thirteen attended to the master's ablutions: one to file the corns on his veiny feet, another to comb the filaments of long colourless hair, one to sharpen the nails, another to shave and powder the powder-white skin, one to pick clean the tiny sharp teeth, another to trim any errant wisps of nose and ear hair, one to place upon bony left fingers rings set with stones of jet, another to place upon bony right fingers rings set with stones of moonwhite, one to place the earring with large stone of crystal in the left ear, one to remove the night's white attire, another to dress him whitely for the day, and one more to oversee it all and to flatter the master.

When all was done, two more served the master a breakfast of coldmeats, whitebread and chilled wine. He ate rapidly. With voracious appetite. And when he was done, his hands were wiped clean by one servant, his mouth dabbed with white napkin by another.

Somewhere else a silver whistle blew.

"Good day, Sir," they trumpeted in unison.

And as they came, so they departed.

"Yes, it is," he said to no one.

"Morrrtttoooooon!" a first voice wheezed.

"Cooorrrneeeliiiuuussssssssss!" a second voice whispered.

"Wiiinnnttteeer!" a third whined.

"Yes, my dears," he said vaguely.

"Time, Morrrtttoooooon!"

"It'ssssss time, Cooorrrneeeliiiuuussssssssss!"

"Oh, yessss! Wiiinnnttteeer! Time!"

And together their whispering, wheezing, whining made a furious sibilant echo.

"Ask nicely, my dears!" He waved a bony, beringed left finger at the empty air.

"Oh, please, Morrrtttoooooon!"

"We beg you, Cooorrrneeeliiiuuussssssssss!"

"We beseech you, Wiiinnnttteeer!"

He clapped his slim hands sharply. "All right, then. To Tabula, it is!"

The room filled with hissing, gleeful laughter as Morton Cornelius Winter leapt to the left corner of the antechamber of his castle.

There it sat. Covered with cloth wrought of silver. His lovely. His beloved. His gift. Awaiting his touch. His cool fingers. Damp palms.

He touched the drape reverently. Swept it off with a whisper. Sighed like a lover at her beauty.

"Tabula," he breathed.

"Assssssk her, Morrrtttoooooon!"

"Assssssk, Cooorrrneeeliiiuuussssssssss!"

"Assssssk her, Wiiinnnttteeer!"

"Enough!" he sniped. And their rustling stilled.

He looked into the obsidian pulchritude of her face. Her pure unadulterated face. And saw his own.

"Speak, my beauty. My Tabula." His breath fogged the blackness.

Sometimes she would not. Oh, she was a willful mistress. Sometimes he would stare stubbornly, longingly at himself hour upon hour. Finally, in frustration, he would quit the corner, pace about the room. He might try again, in angst. In anger. She would not be willed to reply.

Other times she was quick to come. And her face, her voice would draw him into her. He would feast on her food of thought. Her words bewitched him. He would listen to her siren song the daylong until he collapsed, and the servants led him weakly to bed.

Sometimes she was brief. Abrupt. The meanest of replies to his inquiries. A mere affirmation or negation. Then she would turn away. And he would know that was all she would say. Despite his entreaties. Conceits. Fancy words. His sycophancy.

And other times, she would appear and then vanish. Eluding him. He would pound her with his fist. Then instantly regret his violence. Oh, he would plead. He would promise. He would weep. But to no avail. The lady would not heed. Sometimes not for weeks.

And then Morton Cornelius Winter would turn ugly. Drink himself into a stupor. Or sniff until delirious the cold white substance he called snow. He was erratic. Unpredictable. Unseemly. The servants trembled when in this state he beckoned them. His orders were frosty. His commands cruel. Irrational. Sometimes their lives were forfeit as he awaited the black stone's forgiveness.

But it always came. She was, after all, a forgiving mistress. A perfect mistress. Unblemished. Unfailing at last. She spoke to him. And he bathed in her absolution.

This day he knew she would come at his bidding. She had been sullen and silent seven days. But this Monday he felt surely in his bones. He placed his palms upon her. His pale cheek to her.

"Tabula, my darling, speak to me." His thin, pursed lips brushed her black visage.

A murmur began from very far off. It grew into a soft whirring of indistinct words. Louder. A chorus of voices rising, rising to cacophony. Morton Winter covered his ears, squeezed his eyes, held his breath. Then a solitary female voice burst through the crescendo. And all else quieted.

"Ask what you will, Morton Winter."

"Oh, Tabula. Knowing, kind mistress. You grace me with your presence."

The stone table was silent.

"I ask that you grant me news of my kingdom, my vessels, my wealth, today, this finest of Monday mornings as we near my fondest of seasons."

"Morton Winter. This morn your life is not as rich as you would wish. Two of your prizes were thieved seven nights hence."

The thin man took a step back, then peered sharply into the shimmering black surface. "What?"

"From the village Mülle, gone is the woman you sought to tame." The Tabula showed Morton Winter a scene of escape enacted. A dark man, a dark woman, a decoy. Empty stocks.

"Stupid villagers! I'll have the mayor's thumbs in screws! She was to be brought to me! She was to be brought this very morn!"

"And from your own castle, gone is the child."

"NO! It cannot be! The guards assured me the locks were secure! The Sprïggen dungeons impenetrable."

"The locks were secure, the dungeons less so," the black voice spoke calmly. "Observe."

As before, the Tabula presented a vision of what had passed. Flaming hair. A ginger cat. The bars parting as if melting. Child and creature gone in a blink of eye.

Morton Winter tore himself away from the obsidian teller. He circled back twice to convince himself of what he saw. The room grew chilly. Placing a skinny, shaking hand on either side of her face, he spoke through gritted teeth, spittle spattering the black surface. "Who? Where are they?"

No sound. No stirring. He waited.

"Tabula, my darling." His voice was soft, lethal. "Tell on. Who? Where? So I might find these out and punish them. If only to protect you, my dearest one."

Silence. Stillness.

"Tabula," he half-cried. "Fail me not."

"Morton Winter, I know not."

"It—it cannot be. You know all."

"I know not. Something. Someone blurs the knowing."

"MAGIC! I smell magic! Working its malice against me! Against what is mine! I will know who is the mage! The witch! The sorceror! I will know!!"

At this, the Tabula face went blank. In a passion, the angry Winter drew the drape over the stone and stormed towards the silver rope. There he paused, stroking his thin, crooked chin.

"Morrrtttoooooon, what will you do?"

"Cooorrrneeeliiiuuusssssssss, whom do you call?"

"Wiiinnnttteeer, what is your plan?"

"Silence! Away with you! All three! I've had enough of you! Begone!"

Instantly, the room was cool and quiet.

A servant knocked.

"What do you want?"

"Only to stoke the fire, Sir," came a timid voice.

"Leave me!"

Anxious footsteps scuttled away.

Lost in thought, the man, Morton Winter, reached out a skeletal hand. He grasped the cord. Pulled it twice. Then walked towards the dais opposite. Mounted the three steps and sank into the plush cushions of his great silver throne just as the anticipated knock sounded.

"Come."

"Master and My Lord." A hunchbacked form bowed low.

"Rise. And tell me news of the child in the dungeon."

"She is as always. Petulant. Asking incessantly to speak with the Master of the place. Unrelenting. Awaiting your pleasure."

"She is?"

"Yes, Master."

"You saw her yourself. Today. Did you, hmmm?"

The misshapen man would not meet Morton Winter's eyes. "My Lord… I…"

"Did you?"

"My Lord. I confess. I have not yet seen the child this day."

"And yesterday?"

"Milord?"

"Or the day before? Or three days before? When last did you set eyes on the child?"

"Master… We… I made sure daily the child was fed."

"But ne'er once in seven days looked you into her face?"

"My Lord, I confess no. But I will go to her at once."

"Indeed? Well, then you will find her gone." Morton Winter's voice was ice.

"Gone?" His twisted mouth opened in shock.

"Gone, Didion. Idiot! Was she not guarded? Was she not secured?"

"My Lord, yes! We took every precaution. I saw to it personally."

"That must have been my error. It seems clear that you have forgotten why it is I keep you alive." He spat his disgust into a nearby spittoon.

"Master, I forget nothing. Only allow me to investigate this matter immediately."

"Go. And when you return in a moment as you must, knowing nothing more, bring with you the dwarf."

"Yes, my Master and my Lord."

Morton Winter stormed silently on his silver throne. His talon nails pricked the fabric of the cushions in frustration, and his chalky face paled even further in fury. Who had done this to him? Who dared? So be it. This enemy had made a first move against him. Now Morton Winter was ever more resolved to rid Hinterlünd of magic, except for his express purposes and under his careful and tight control. Firm and certain, he would have all magic, all knowledge within his grip.

And when he found these interlopers, these thievish ne'er-do-wells, he would devise a punishment befitting the crime. Hot wax perhaps, although that was growing stale. Perhaps the item of Winter's own design that the dwarf had been working on in his smithy. He shivered in anticipation.

Another knocked smartly at the door.

"Come."

"Master. I bring you the guards. And the dwarf." Didion's voice filled the room.

"Say what you know," Morton Winter barked at the two burly men.

"M-m-my M-m-master, I saw naught. Only now, when Didion bade me, did I looksee and find the girlchild gone."

"I- I, too, m'Lord."

Two bulks grovelled, shaking before the silver throne.

"Methinks witchcraft is abroad," the first mumbled.

"Ah. You think. Do not think, idiot. Work! You were to do your jobs. Stay awake. Alert. Where were you? A'gaming? Drinking rotgut ale? Whoring at the brothel. What lured you from your posts?"

"Nay, m'Lord," insisted the first. "We were at our posts each nightlong! We ne'er strayed nor slept."

"Silence, imbecile!" Winter's voice ricocheted between the antechamber walls. "Get out! And Didion, ensure that these receive their due reward for their efforts."

The three exited, Didion bowing.

"And now, Dagnott."

"Master." The lumpish, short fellow drew nearer the dais.

"Didion has told you what mischief has befallen us?"

"Aye. He told."

"Go forth alone and find the churls who stole my jewels. Bring them hither. You have one fortnight."

"But a fortnight, Lord?"

"A fortnight. The hated Yule will too soon be upon us. The culprits' scent and tracks will be lost then in the snow."

The dwarf considered Winter's words in silence.

"Know you where your son is, Dagnott?"

"No, Master." Dagnott's voice spelled misery.

"I know one who knows." Winter leaned forward. "And so may you." The dwarf met his gaze. "Upon your return."

"Aye, my Lord. I heed your words."

"Go. Leave on the morrow. No! Better still. Hie you thence this day!"

Dagnott quitted the chamber, leaving Winter alone, mired in his thoughts.

The day grew dim. Morton Winter left the dais and moved to the crystal decanters glinting near his bedstead. He poured himself a goblet of the clear distilled liquid. Drank it down. Poured another. Wandered the room. Looked out the frosted panes. Within the hour, and after four such goblets, a servile knock at the door announced his dinner.

At Winter's frosty bidding, the platoon of white-clad servants re-entered the ante chamber. Now several set about lighting the sconces set in the walls, the candles on the tables, while two others stoked and fed the dying fire. Two helped him dress for dinner in a silver silk brocade smoking jacket, while a third brushed and dressed his thin, gossamer hair back into a tail. One anointed him with cologne, while another placed a large silver amulet shaped like a crystal of snow about his neck. Six set the grand table near the fireplace: one set linens, one china, one crystal, one a spoon, fork and knife. A seventh stood poised to pull out the master's chair. The wine steward offered the evening's selections, uncorked the master's choice, and poured. The poison taster tasted, fell writhing in agony. Two hefty servants bore the dead body away.

"You!" the master commanded an anonymous servant near his elbow.

Terrified, the man watched the wine steward uncork a second bottle and pour, handing him the glass. He drank. And lived. The master's glass was filled.

Nine dinner servants lined the walls, holding aloft the covered dishes for the evening repast. As each course was tested for poison then served, each attendant would return to his place and resume the vigil until the last morsel was consumed and a nearby servant had wiped clean the master's blue lips.

"Brrrrrrrrrp!" Morton Winter was satisfied. He had dined well.

At this signal, a servant pulled back his chair, while the table clearers set to work in a flurry. At the pillow tossed divan, another awaited to plump the cushions and assist Morton Winter to recline. His sychophant attended the master's selection for the evening entertainment, as the dinner servants exited the room, smartly and timely.

"Bring the Rowan slave girl to dance for me, the Piedmont piper and drummer, and my fool." A servant refilled Winter's goblet as the master sank into the evening.

Moments later the musicians and dancer were assembled, the fool on a bench to the left of the divan. The piper struck up a melody, which elsewhere would have been merry, and his compatriot drummed along. The Rowan dancer, a slight girl of about fourteen, danced cheerlessly before Winter. When the tune ended, she sank to the floor.

Winter's chafing humour persisted. "This. This was no dance. Merely motion. This music? This music must needs improve if you value those nimble fingers. Now! Fool! Tell us a jest or two."

The motley-clad figure rose to his feet and eyed the glazed-eyed Winter. "Sweetmeats give goodtaste; but liquor makes posthaste."

"Ha! That is certain. Liquor makes posthaste, indeed. And you, slave-girl make posthaste to this chaise."

In three quick steps, the dark skinned maiden was beside him. She had learned well the stinging lesson of the whip.

"Steward, pore the wench a goblet and fill mine. A riddle perhaps, Fool?"

The jester delayed, scratching his head.

"Fool, I'm in an icy humour!"

"Master, we are all of us frozen aware."

"Ha!"

"This then my riddle. I am cold in my airiest, cold in my nether regions. Hoarfrost for heart, icicles for spleen. Ha'frozen in life; ha'frozen in death. Say what I am."

Morton Winter drank deeply from his goblet. He looked into its crystal pattern. Then suddenly sent it soaring past the jester's left ear, smashing into the fireplace.

"Get out!"

"My riddle needs an answer!"

"Get out! I know the answer. The answer is winter! But you play foolish on words to imply Morton Winter! Get out! Get out before I cut out your snide, mocking tongue from your useless head. Out, I say!" He threw a piece of fruit at the laughing form dashing from the room.

Morton Winter next lurched at the girl. But tonight her revulsion repulsed him. "You, too. Wench. Out! Get out! Teach her and the fool some manners," he called after the swiftly departing and fawning mainservant.

Another obsequient helped him to shaky feet and over to the bedstead where a fellow already worked at heating the bed with bedwarmer. Winter pushed aside the basin of tepid water one man brought, but relieved himself in the chamber pot an assistant held before him. The testy master sent insults at two who dressed him in nightclothes, swore at a final, who helped him into bed and covered him. Three last remaining snuffed the sconces and candles, poked the fire. The door locked after their collective retreat.

"Good e'en, Morton," sighed his right slipper from beneath the great, wayward bed.

"Good e'en, Morton," echoed the left, in muffled voice.

"Sssleep well, Morrrtttoooooon!" a first voice wheezed against the latticed window.

"Sssleep tight, Cooorrrneeeliiiuuusssssssss!" a second voice whispered down the fireplace chimney.

"Sssleep deep, Wiiinnnttteeer!" a third whined at the shutter.

"Ssshut up!" Morton slurred. And his snores sliced the crisp night.

CHAPTER

"Orange hair, orange hair,
Unaware that I stare
At your orange hair, orange hair."

HER SINGSONG VOICE SOFTLY MOCKED. The child touched the hair of the sleeper and thought about pulling it. Just a strand or two loose. But that would be mean-spirited. And this 'she' had saved her. Better to make a good first impression. There would be time enough for this 'she' to hate her. As they all did, eventually. When they knew.

She slipped gingerly from the bedclothes and her bed. Around the orange-haired reclining on the floor-pallet beside her. She felt shaky from her week's illness. The air was chill and her rags-for-clothes gone. A green cloak on a peg would do. She pulled the fabric close about her, hoisted the hem to avoid tripping.

Spying food and cupboards, the child crossed the reed-mat floor. Six deft fingers. And a large crust of bread found its way up her right sleeve. Six more and a dry rind of cheese up the left, while an apple found her mouth. Then into a pair of too-large boots, and out the door.

It was cold, but she had been much colder. She gorged herself on bread and cheese, trying not to choke. Broke the thin scale of ice atop the rain barrel water, dipped cupped hands to drink, dried her hands on the cloak. The weakness in her limbs forced her to sit on the tree stump next the barrel. Already chilled, she munched the apple and stared about her.

A thatched cottage within a circle of trees. A crescent moon painted above the door. A small garden, frost-ruined. A path northwards through the trees. A cart trail southwards. A circle of stones about the margins. Curious. Who was this 'she'?

"Ingamald." The voice at the now-open door startled the child so that she dropped her apple. Witch and child watched it roll away into the sear grass and muck. "Leave it for the birds. Come into Nookeshea. Into the cottage and draw near the fire. What I have is yours. There is food a'plenty. And therefore no need to steal it."

Sheepishly, the child did as bidden. Removed the boots. Finally brought her eyes up to meet the bemused gaze of her hostess who had closed and bolted the door.

"That is my cloak, and you are welcome to it until I must leave for market where I will buy you something more akin to your size."

The child, embarrassed, sniffed.

"Come to the fire. See here. I have brought the coals to life!"

She dragged herself, the cloak trailing behind her, towards a three-legged stool at the hearth and sat. A black sinewy form slinked towards her out of the shadows.

"Ayi!"

"Be not afraid. This is Beezle. Friend and familiar."

The child shrank back.

"Heed not the foolish lore about black cats. Beezle will not harm you. See how he purrs and rubs. He craves your friendship."

With tentative hand, the child reached out. Beezle, eager for affection, rubbed sleek cat ears and face against her palm.

"Aye, that's it. And now you know what we are called. What is your name?"

"Some call me Yda."

"A good name. What do others?"

"Mongrel. Mischief. Bastard. And worse."

"These are ugly and ill-fitting. You are none of these."

Yda shivered. "Whereat are we?"

"We are in Brüe Wood and in my cottage Nookeshea. While with me, you are safe from harm's way."

"They will find me. Again."

"Well. You are here in secret. And I keep secrets tightly in my safekeeping."

Yda remembered the daring night escape. A cat become woman. She eyed Ingamald nervously. "What are you?"

"A witch." Ingamald stirred the cauldron over the fire. The child gulped and held her peace.

"Fear not. This is no witch's brew I stir, but broth for our midday meal." She ladled two bowls, one for herself and one for the child, and placed the crockery on the small table. To this repast she added bread, cheese and a jug of milk. "Come. Eat. You have nothing on your bones."

Yda tripped to the table and sat across from Ingamald on a straw-bottomed chair. Although she had just eaten, she ate greedily again, slurping noisily from the bowl and afterwards licking it out. She did not take her eyes from the witch through the entire meal.

"Did they not feed you?"

"Sometimes. Somat. Other times, no."

"What did they want of you?"

Yda shrugged and stuffed her mouth with bread. She would not tell this she-witch aught. Leastwise, not now.

Ingamald sighed. "Stand please, and let me look on you."

Yda rose a little unsteadily and clasped her hands behind her back.

"I needs must attend the length of your arms, so hold them out."

Yda shook her head.

"Yda," Ingamald's voice was gentle. "I know already about the six and six."

Resignedly, the child held out both arms, gooseflesh rising on her skin.

Ingamald measured her with a careful eye. "For me and mine, six is a number of good fortune. It is a witchy number. I like it well."

The child looked closely at her hands. "Six has ever been my undoing."

"Now it is your luck."

Ingamald cleared the bowls to the small sideboard and wiped clean the pine table. She filled a cracked bowl with the remainder of the milk for Beezle who abandoned his bath by the fire in favour of quick milkish consumption. Yda chuckled. It was the first time she had smiled in a great, long time. Ingamald noted the sweet features of her charge as her own witch fingers worked her copper hair into a braid.

"Now you must surrender my cloak, for I must swiftly to the village and to market. I will return within two hours." She swept the deep green cloak about her shoulders with a flourish, then bent and took Yda's firmly in her hands. "I know you are fearful. I see flight in your eyes. But should you stray beyond the circle of stones that secure this house from the sight of your enemies, you will be again in grave danger. I know not how to win your trust, Yda. But believe you, I, Ingamald, am your friend. Here now. Take this woolen for your comfort to wear until my return."

Yda nodded, gathering the shawl about herself. This 'she' could penetrate her very thoughts, and it unnerved the child.

"Will I find you here when I return?" Ingamald arched her left brow.

"Aye."

"Good then. Lock the door behind me. You will know my knock when I return."

"Howso?"

"I will knock six and six," smiled Ingamald.

And with a flash of copper she was gone. Yda slid the heavy bolt in place. Turned and surmised the room. It was simple, as were most of the dwellings she had ever known. Warm and windsafe. Yda added another log to the fire and listened to the satisfying crackle as it caught aflame. She wandered to the pegs of clothing. Simple homespun. And something else softer than her child's skin. Skirt and blouse. In hues she had never before seen. What need had the 'she' of these fine clothes? Her child's curiosity drew her over to another small table atop of which sat an open book, hugely half her size. She turned the pages and puzzled at the figures. Yda could read and write, knowledge that had been a source of suspicion. But these markings were strange to her. They moved on the page; they addled her thoughts. She turned away from the text in half-fear and half-frustration. Much about this 'she' was strange.

If a witch, why still alive? Why still free? How had the 'she' escaped? How had the 'she' changed from woman to cat to woman? Was the answer in the odd book?

Yda scowled at her reflection in the window. Gradually her brow unfurrowed as she surrendered to her waking dreams. Like so much in her life, such dreaming by day was an act of self-preservation. Someday, she longed for a someone who would hear her thoughts and know.

Know all the secret and wonderful thoughts of a girl but ten and one. A girl who knew things. Who could read and write. A girlchild who was different. A girlchild who could make things happen. Special things. Magic things. Like bending her brother Hugh's sickle as it sat waiting for its dayswork. Just using her thoughts. Her special and secret mindthoughts. Yes, she was special. Even though others did not say it. They knew it. And in fear and envy, threw stones. Called her names. Ripped her hair out. Tackled her. Beat her blue. Even so. And despite. Yda was a special girlchild. Touched, her mother once spake afore she died of plague. A girlchild with six fingers on each adroit hand.

And what crafty fingers. They beat her sisters at Cat's Cradle. They thrummed rhythmically the drum. A more steady and hypnotic beat than her thick brothers could muster when the 'hes' were a'making music. Fingers that deftly threaded the needle to sew the six and twenty stitches on Hugh's leg, the day the crooked sickle had slipped to cut he. Yda's fault. And she was sorry for it. So she made her six fingers sew neatly and surely. There would be but a trace of the cut once healed.

Aye, she was sorry for Hugh. But not always with remorse for the other accidents. Yda lifted her chin proudly. Defiantly. A six-fingered girlchild had to outwit her enemies.

Goody Loman was the first in the village. Her first enemy. Her first real victim.

A vain woman, proud and haughty. And her children just like she. These called Yda "scamp" and pushed her aside. Once Goody Loman took a broom to Yda's bottom when the girl came peering into the Loman great house of Loman Village. All Yda wanted was a cup of water to curb her thirst of a dogday afternoon.

So Yda watched. Waited for her chance. Goody Loman had great yellow curls that she prized highly. Yda knew that Goody Loman washed and brushed and played with these curls. While the servants worked, the woman primped.

It was easy really. A simple song. A mind-picture of Goody's curls falling limp and lustreless. And it was done.

Yda knew well enough to stay out of sight. The spoiled woman shrieked for days. Tried repeatedly to redress her hair. Cried witch at the old woman beggar in the village. Swore to have her whipped. Yda held her breath. This the girl did not foresee. But the crone disappeared before caught. And Yda was unrepentant. Goody Loman's locks were forever lost. Good riddance.

And so it was for hurts and slights the girl received from her peers, her siblings, her father. Time upon time. Over many lonely years. Especially since her Mama died. If Papa beat her, he would find his best pipe with knotted stem. If her sisters chastised, their needles would bend uselessly while they stitched. If Toord or the other Loman village bratlings teased or spat, their horseshoes would contort, their javelins crook midplay. No one knew for sure whence these powers sprang, but most cast their suspicions upon the twelve-fingered girl who could make letters and read them.

When the edict came, it was most natural for Yda to be one of the first arrested. Her own brother, Bose, took her by hand to the jaoler.

Well, Bose since had his own misery. His blacksmith's hammer cracked midthrow, tossing up an unlucky horseshoe, burning and maiming him for life. And so, poor poor lad. Jess the miller's fetching daughter now took no more interest in Bose's favours.

Until this time these were private reveries for her alone. Could Yda trust this Ingamald? The she-witch had will-bent open the dungeon bars which Yda herself could not move, not knowing their owner. Surely then, this 'she' had even greater power and no need of Yda's own. And further, this 'she' had promised to keep a freakish secret safe. Whyso if she only willed Yda harm? Mayhaps it was safe to trust this one. It had been a long time since Yda's last trusting. Not since the Bookewoman. And before, not since her mother.

A knock sounded six times on the door. A pause. Another six rappings. Yda flew to the bolt, and in swept Ingamald, colour at her cheeks from the chill wind.

Laughing. "Yda. You are still here!"

"Aye." The girl watched the witch decloak, drop several parcels, and warm herself before the fire.

"What have you been about these near two hours, Yda?"

"Whimsy."

"E'en so? Good for you. I, myself, am prone to whimsy." Ingamald glanced to a broom in the corner. "And flights of fancy." Her hands soothed, she offered to Yda a knotted bundle. "A gift. For Yda."

"F-for Yda?" The child took tentative hold of the sack. Then tore into it with a flying of dexterous fingers. "Ahh!" Within was a complete set of clothes. Shift, stockings, woolen skirt of rich wine hue and a shawl to match. Two Yda-sized boots of black leather. She let slip the woolen to the floor and pounced upon the clothes. In a moment, Ingamald was measuring and tucking.

"But a stitch here and here. How fit those boots?"

Yda skipped about the cottage.

"Made for Yda

made for Yda

Bootie black boots for Yda, Yda!"

"Hark! The lass sings as a lark!" Ingamald clapped her hands as Yda repeated her refrain. She turned to stoke the fire as the girl's dance enlivened Nookeshea.

"Ingamald."

"Aye."

The wicca woman kept her back to the timid voice.

"Thankee."

"It was naught, child."

"I mean, thankee for Yda's rescue, too."

Ingamald turned then to look at the girl. "I would not leave you to such cruelty. And all because you have fingers six and six."

"It is more than that they fear."

"Aye?"

"Aye. I have a power, too."

"Ah. I wondered."

"I can bend somethings. Move somethings."

Ingamald arched an eyebrow. "Then why not did you bend the bars of your own cage?"

"Only the somethings of the someones I know."

The witch nodded. "Here then. This is my fork. Crook'd tines it had when I bought it for a sale. Can you make them straight anew?"

"I can. I will." And Yda commenced singing:

"Fork with tines askew

Make all straight anew!"

Three tines trembled at her singsong voice. And when they stilled, were straight.

For a second time, Ingamald clapped her hands. "Oh, Yda! What a gift is this!"

"Why could not you straighten your own fork?"

Ingamald picked the tool up and examined it closely. "I meant to straighten it with my own hands and perhaps a hammer."

"Nay. I mean, why not with your magic?"

"Magic is not for whim. It is a serious art. A sacred practice. It needs must be exercised in reverence. And only when there is need. Why fix with magic what I can with my bare hands? Just because it is easy to use the craft to remove what thwarts us? Nay. That is not for magic. Magic is for need, not play."

"Then you have never made magic for sport?"

Ingamald thought back to another firelit room six years ago before she left the safety of Hana's cottage in Hören Wood. A dancing poppit. Magic sands. A charmed old woman.

"Aye. I have. For play and entertainment. But not to find what my wits could themselves divine, nor to change what should not be changed, neither to profit from the way of wicca."

"Wicca?"

"The craft. Witchcraft. I do not, nor do those I respect, use witchcraft for gain. Or to stop the rains. Halt the winds. Forego the snows. Those things must be for life to prosper."

"But. Sometimes the rains go on and on. Sometimes the weak succumb in winter."

"All true. But who am I to fight Nature's ways? The Great Mother knows aught. She knows what she is about. And I will not meddle in her affairs with magic. That would be to work against her, whom I trust and revere."

"But this is just a fork! Whom do you harm in straightening?"

The witch laughed. "Aye, but a fork. To straighten would harm none. But I have these two able hands to straighten. Or a new friend to do the favour for me! Best to save my own magic for more important, more befitting tasks."

Yda smiled shyly back at her.

"Now tell me your story, child of Loman Village."

"H-how did you know my village?"

The witch shrugged and smiled. "Magic," she teased.

As the afternoon wore on into evening, Yda told. All that she had endured since the death of her mother, the person who best loved her. The subsequent treatment of her indifferent and surly father. Her jealous and fearful siblings. The villagers who looked at her with mistrust and loathing. The children who made her feel a freak. The cruel edict from some someone new in charge who sent orders via Ruheplatz to seek out freaks. Imprison and condemn them. A someone who wanted something from Yda.

"Morton Winter," sighed Ingamald.

"That is the 'he's' name?" Yda tucked that knowledge away for later.

She continued to tell Ingamald about her revenge upon her tormentors. The witch frowned but said nothing. When Yda finished telling about the treatment she received at the hands of her captors, the two had finished their supper and sat before the fire. Beezle was a curl of fur in Yda's lap.

Yda's voice was hoarse. "Now. Your telling. I have told you mine."

And so Ingamald wove the tale of her life. Stitched the story of her bewitching childish ways, her subsequent abandonment on old witch Hana's doorstep by her foster father. Followed the thread of her banishment from Hören Wood, her leaving of Hana in the witch girl's sixteenth summer. Cross-stiched the ugly learning of her mother's wickedness: a magical tapestry that wove itself and tried thus to weave a terrible, destructive fate for Ingamald and all of Hinterlünd. Woven in amongst this impending peril, her meeting of the village goodwife, Sall, and the healing of her daughter. Ingamald's capture by the Musica who became dear friends, and the Troubadour who was something more. Her waking kiss that brought back to life Prince Ranðulfr of Ruheplatz. Her escape from two dastardly highwaymen and happy discovery of Nookeshea, this cottage wherein she spun this tale. And finally, when her witchy voice grew hoarse, Ingamald tied the disparate knots together with her meeting of Spinne, sorceress mother who wished to transform Hinterlünd into a wasteland of misery. Except that Ingamald devoured the dreaded witch, just as in the folktales.

Yda listened, started, gasped at various of the details. When the last stitch of Ingamald's tapestry story was knotted, Yda looked at the witch in admiration and awe.

"And you have lived safely hence ever since?"

"Aye," Ingamald frowned. "Mostly in secret. To the detriment of my fellows." Yda looked puzzled. "While I have been safe, many are not so. You, for one."

The girl nodded and whispered, "The Bookewoman."

"Who?"

"A f-friend. She is gone. I know not where."

"There are many like her, I fear. But we have a plan."

"We?"

"We rebels. A band of outcasts like yourself. And we mean to undo this evil. To undo Morton Winter."

Yda shivered. "Howso?"

"That will be determined on the morrow, I believe. When the Troubadour, his sister and fire-eater Ingo come to call. And who knows who else?"

"Those all to come?"

"Indeed. And that means you and I must rest early this night. Tomorrow will be a day of much ado."

The wicca woman and the girl prepared for bed. Ingamald tucked her charge into the soft cot and sought the bedmat beside her. Beezle purred near her ear.

"Ingamald?" Yda's drowsy voice roused the witch from near-slumber. "Wherever will you put everyone?"

"That Yda," Ingamald smiled, "is a very good question."

CHAPTER

A SUDDEN LURCH of wheel tossed her from dream. She stayed awake, this time not succumbing again to exhaustion as with her other wakings. In the darkness, she did not dread. Warm beneath eiderdown. Safe. That was all she knew. Except that she was long removed from the cruel taunts and mistreatment of the Mülle villagers, those who had burned her books and threatened to burn her.

And she'd had little doubt that, at the slightest provocation, they would indeed light their hungry torches and set aflame her hair, her clothes, herself. So she had kept mum. And awake—barely—for a day and a night and a day. Until that night. The night of the liberators. She did not know whether they were truly liberators or mercenaries or emissaries from the great enemy. She did not now know how many nights ago she had been freed. Now, safe under the coverlet in the rolling covered cart, she neither cared nor wondered. She was merely grateful to be free, if only for this one warm night.

Lira's right side was bruised, and so she turned gingerly to her left. She could make nothing out in the shadows. It must be deep night. There were sounds of horses. Creaking of the wagon. An occasional whisper or single whistle. Other than that, the going was quiet. Surely these, too, were at great pains to be undiscovered by the man, Morton Winter. Otherwise, why this night journey, hasty and covert?

The cartwheel struck a boulder, and she winced in pain. One pain reminded her of another. Her man. Her girlchild, Oonagh. Both dead of pox. It struck sure and swift. Leaving her to wonder why she alone of her small family still lived.

There had followed a time when everything was dull. The things that had meant something—the cleanness of the laundry, the daily walk on errands, the quiet, tidy house—lost importance. And she tried to go through the days, will her way through the greyness of living on when a husband and child are lost. But like winter clouds, thick and unyielding, the fog in her brain and of her life would not lift.

And then. The day she wandered lonely into market and found the Bookeseller. Astride a three-legged stool next an open cart of dusty, ancient books.

"Want a bit o' a read, then, do ye?" A hoarse voice roused Lira from her stupor.

"I don't know. I…"

"Can read, can't ye? From the looks of yer finery and soft hands. Ye come from having, that's what!"

"Y-yes. It's true. I read. We had books."

"Had?"

"Have. Some. Somewhere." Lira's brow furrowed. She felt dazed by this woman's questions.

"Somat. Some'er. Don't ye know that books be treasure? Reading and knowledge magic?"

"I…"

"Well, don't stand stupid. Pick out a text or two."

Lira chose randomly. This strange woman discomfited her.

"Let's have a looksee. Oh, what a pretty one!" The crone pointed to the blue tattered cover, careworn and oft-fingered. "That's a fine booke. Popular, too. I'm sure the Miss will fancy such a tale."

"Missus."

The aged woman eyed her. "Missus, is it? Well, then, Missus t'is. That booke be yers until next we meet. Give it me back again… or if ye've another, I'll take it in trade."

"Until next time? But when?" Lira did not recollect this seller before.

"Don't ye be afeared. There is always a next time once I set me eyes on a word-lover. I'll find ye!" And she burst into a cacophonous cackle and wheeled away her small barrow cart.

When Lira blinked, there was no trace of the Bookewoman. No dust. No track in the dirt from the wheels of her covered barrow. She glanced at the title in her hands: *The Strange but Goodish Adventures of a Younge Missus, Her Passing Griefs and Sorrows and How She Came to Peace Through Good Works and Good Bookes.*

Over the weeks, she read the text six times, and each time, somehow, the reading was different. Words changed themselves, rearranged themselves on the page. She turned to the book first for her comfort. Then next reading the words offered guidance. With the third and fourth, serenity and calm. Followed by peace and consolation. And finally a measuring of her days to come. Each time she read, Lira felt the presence of the Bookewoman. A kind of trance befell her as she turned the pages. She often sat through an entire day, text in hand, until it toppled to the floor as she slipped into dreams. The pain of her losses did not leave her, but grew softer around the edges. Lira turned her face to the sun and learned anew how to smile at life.

And to think again beyond herself. She kept the original book, but brought another volume to market one day on a whim. And there was she, the Bookewoman, in the same spot as those many months before. This time Lira asked the woman to sup at her fine family home near the river.

The Bookewoman ate with great appetite and few manners. She burped and farted unself-consciously in Lira's presence, as if in praise and appreciation. Lira found herself laughing. Often. And the

Bookewoman joined in raucously.

"Now then that I've found ye. Here is what ye're to do."

"Pardon?"

"Ye know. Now 'at yer life be at peace. Or nearly so. I grow old, I do. I'm a needin' ye. And I've been a'watchin' ye. Sure, t'is you have the words and a way with 'em. Ye come from luck and fortune's circumstance, that's what. Time's now for to be givin' out somat of what ye've been a' given."

"I- I..."

"Don't stand with yer mouth a' gapin. Flies or worse'll take residence. Now then, I need ye well, don't I? Not floppin' or fallin' from the plague."

"What is it you would have me do?"

"Why sell the bookes, ye silly git! What did ye think? Work the brothel?" And the ancient one burst into a laughing and coughing fit.

"Sell the books?"

"Aye. Towne to towne. City to city. Port to port. Sell when ye can. Give when ye must. Or when there's need. If ye run out, I'll replenish. Or one o' mine will. Sure, ye'll have nae shortage o' bookes ever."

"One of yours?"

"Aye. The Learneds. Welcome to the Learneds, lass. It's a special company. A secret sistership and fellowship. And ye're a one o' us."

"I am?"

"Ha! By those very words, ye are!"

"Just like that!'

"Just the like!"

Incredulous, but agreeable, Lira joined. Took up a life anew. Knowing nothing about being a Learned, only that she was to travel with books in tow, wherever books were needed. And according to the Bookewoman, that was everywhere.

A year and a bit passed. Lira read and passed along many a book. She gave to children. To simple village schools. Families. To those who could not read, Lira read. To the sick. The old. The blind.

She taught letters to youngsters and goodwives. And she passed on through village and town. City and port. In a year and a bit, Lira learned the geography of Hinterlünd. And as the second year wore on, she learned of the man, Morton Winter, from the other Learneds who passed her cart and horse on the road, or set up bookeshoppe beside her from time to time, or sent sealed letters to her. Until it got dangerous and seals were broken. Carts overturned. Booksellers beaten. Books burned. Her fellows and sisters grew cautious. Frightened. They hid then.

But not Lira. Foolish or brave, she went forth. Children depended on her. Citizens missed her. She had a job. A vocation. A calling. And although she had not seen the Bookewoman for six month or more, Lira knew in her bones that despite the dangers, the old woman trundled onwards with her barrow. Somewhere. Somehow. And so would Lira.

Until the ugliness in Mülle. Her arrest. The ignorant masses. Those very same she had sought to inform, turned informants. Took her books. Her beautiful books. Turned them to ashes. Tears stung her eyes.

A hooting sound startled her from these thoughts. Owl or human? She listened. But heard only the babbling of a brook. Smelled a sour marsh smell. Recognized a scraping of branches against the sides of the wagon. And then all motion stopped. She heard the jingling of horses unhitching. Soft voices. Wind in trees.

Her eyelids grew heavy in the stillness. And unknowing, Lira slipped back into unknowing.

Roc silently loosed the arrow from the taut bow. Replaced it in his quiver. He gazed with sharp night vision into the circle of stones where the caravan and travellers had come to rest. These were all asleep. Within the circle of stones. They had to be friends, therefore. The stones permitted no enmity or enemy. He had seen this before. Intruders repelled as an arrow glances off a boulder. So these were friends of the one with the hair of flames. The one with the good medicine. The one he watched over. The one who was guardian of this Bruë Wood. The one who had caught sight of him, wounded. After he had escaped the attack on his family. His people. And he, limping and hurt, came to this safe place. And this one had seen him, even after he ran from her as now he ran from any with white skin. But later that day he found the moss. The healing medicine. And food. Set out for him just outside the stone circle. And Roc bound the moss with leather to his wounds. And they were well in two suns.

So this one could be trusted. She knew he lived in the wood, for when she left him things—a cup, fruit, a woolen blanket in the fall—he, in turn, brought her an occasional hare or fish from the brook. But she did not know he watched her. Or so he hoped. She knew many things, he had come to realize. Which berries were fair, which foul. How to turn brownish water clear. How to read the sun. The stars. He had watched her, unseen. Just as he watched these.

Roc had never spoken to her but wondered if she knew about his people. That they were no more. He alone survived from his forest village to the north. His family. Grandparents. Young wife-to-be. Dead. Gone to join his ancestors. So much sorrow for someone of only twenty winters. Loss licked at his heart. He wondered if the one with burning hair knew. Roc wanted to tell her but held himself back. Still and silent as stone.

These in the circle would not harm her. He slipped soundlessly away and lost himself within the bare birches.

CHAPTER

THE YOUNG WITCH PAUSED before the latticed window, weaving her hair in an intricate copper braid. Through the half-frosted panes she gazed at the two bright caravan wagons at rest within the circle of stones about her place. Relief seeped through her breast.

Beezle stretched himself awake from atop her pallet and slinked over to twist between her ankles. His "mirrrrrrow" posed the unspoken question.

"I do not know what we are doing, Beezle cat." Ingamald bent down to stroke his ears fondly and whisper. "But if you know aught, please say." A feline stare met her emerald eyes, but the cat said nothing.

The witch worked the fireplace embers into a flame and set a huge pot of porridge cooking. She moved close to Yda's sleeping form.

"Yda. Child. It is time. Our first guests have arrived and will be hungry for breakfast."

"Who they?" Yda's voice was hoarse and sleepy.

"My friend, the Troubadour, and I know not who else."

Ingamald resumed stirring the thick mixture in the pot as the child scrambled into her day-old clothes. The witch handed the girl the great spoon and smiled.

"Think you that fingers six and six can keep the porridge from burning?"

"I was cooke for a family of seven before and never ruined a pot." Yda's voice was edged with pride.

"Good then. I'll see to the guests." And swirling the great green cloak about her shoulders, Ingamald left Nookeshea.

Yda stirred quickly. Then crept to the window and saw. Two covered wagons, bright green, gold, and purple. Symbols painted thereon in daring display. A language? Or signs? A door to one swung open and out leapt a dark man who took the witch woman eagerly in his arms and kissed her. So the 'she' had a 'he'. A handsome. Yda wrinkled her nose and took herself back to the fire and her task. She didn't much care for the looks of he.

They entered with a flourish of laughter and flashing of eyes. A small man limped after them, carrying two cases. Still laughing, Ingamald took them from the man.

"Here friend, Capo. Let me lighten your load."

"Away from the fire, if you please, Mistress Ingamald."

She placed the two zantauri cases in the far corner, away from both draft and heat.

The Troubadour gazed on her movements warmly.

Ingamald pulled up chairs for her guests and steered Yda by the shoulders before them. "This is Yda."

The child refused to smile. Refused the Troubadour's proffered hand.

"So. A child saved by a witch." He reached suddenly behind her ear, producing a coin. "It seems you are rich in luck and, it would also seem," he bit the coin to test its worth, "silver".

Yda gasped and clutched the hand with the coin. "Where did you? How did you?"

He with the coin threw back his head and laughed, baring his teeth, one golden to boot.

"This is the Troubadour, Yda. And his companion, Capo. Friends, both. And mayhaps yours."

"Is it mine?" Yda still clutched the hand with the coin.

"Ah. You want I should buy your regard?"

"Nay." Yda eyed him narrowly. "I want the coiny."

The three adults erupted in laughter.

"So. If you want. You must see where the coin goes." And the Troubadour began an elaborate game of switching the coin between his hands. Now he presented the child two closed fists. "Choose, Yda."

"Right!"

The Troubadour opened an empty palm. "Ah, sadly. No, little one. You have lost." He opened the left palm, revealed the coin. Tossed it from hand to hand.

Yda tilted her head sharply. "You tricked me!"

"And you have learned your first Musica lesson."

"What?"

"Not to trust all you think you see." The Troubadour opened his left palm a second time. Empty. And again his right. Empty also.

Yda wondered what injury to cause this 'he.' If she could just manage to melt that golden tooth…

Ingamald's voice interrupted her thoughts. "Do not tease her. Yda has had enough of taunts." The witch spoke calm but certain as she spooned steaming porridge into bowls.

"I do not tease. I teach."

Yda put her hands defiantly on her hips. The Troubadour glanced down at her fingers. She closed them self-consciously, sullenly into fists. "What?"

"Not to judge all one sees." His voice was mild. The Troubadour drew his hand across the shadow of his unshaven face. "Look you under the pillow of your bed and find what you seek."

Doubtfully, Yda backed from him. Slowly towards the bed. Then she turned and lifted the pillow. The coin winked at her from the bedlinen. She took it. Bit it as he had done. It was solid and hurt her teeth. She pocketed the coin. Came back to the three and accepted the bowl of porridge Ingamald set before her. Yda glanced at the Musica 'he' who beamed goldenly at her. She worked hard to keep her mouth from twitching.

Throughout the humble meal, the Troubadour talked quietly. Yda listened, wide-eyed, to a tale of harrowing escape, not unlike her recent own.

"I know nothing about the woman." The Troubadour pushed his empty bowl away. "Erabesque, who saw to her in the caravan, said she was terrified and mute. Since then, I have looked in twice on our refugee, but she slept soundly."

"Then we will hear her tale when she rouses, which looks to be now." Ingamald glanced towards the face at the window. She went to the door and threw it ajar.

"Come in, traveller. We are friends, not foes. Here is fire and food and cheer."

The woman stepped uncertainly towards the doorway. Drawing a wary hand though the tangle of her hair, she put a timid foot upon the threshold.

The party bade her welcome, put a bowl in her hands. Lira found it difficult to return their smiles, embarrassed as she was by her own filth and their attentions. She told them her name, they theirs. She spoke of her village, haltingly about her capture, her captors.

Sensing her discomfort, Ingamald shooed the others from the cottage—the Troubadour and Capo to collect water and cut wood, Yda to gather brush. And so the two women were alone. The witch heated water over the fire, filled a large bathing tub into which Lira tenuously lowered her bruised body. Ingamald helped Lira to wash her hair. Gently, together they cleansed away the grime and smear of the past several days. After a bit of salve was applied to a graze across her face, Lira broke the silence between them.

"Thank you, Mistress."

"Ingamald."

"Ingamald. How did you know of me? Your friends find me?"

"We have our ways. We watch. Wait. Until it is prudent to move. We seek out the persecuted, to save or set free."

"The child was saved also?"

"Aye. She, too. Walled in the very dungeon of the tyrant. Stolen from under his nose." Ingamald chuckled.

"His wrath will triple."

"Aye. As will our efforts. But tell—what is your story?"

And so in the quiet, dressed in borrowed robes, as together the women worked the tangles from Lira's hair, she untangled her tale.

"Then you are a Learned."

"I suppose. Though how I came to be I know not quite. Happenstance and luck."

"This Bookewoman. Is she safe, know you?"

"I hope, but…"

"We will find her whereabouts. Fear not."

Lira turned to admire the shelf of volumes on the wall opposite. "You, too, are a Learned."

"Nay. Merely a witch."

"To them, to him, it is one and the same."

"Aye. So I am told."

Abruptly, the door dashed open. A creature with raven hair and wearing multi-coloured silks—blood red, green envy, and nightsky indigo—whisked in. An exotic sweet scent filled the room now seemingly smaller with this newest occupant.

"Ah. There is she! Our rescued. And Ingamald, sister witch. So. You are still bewitching my only brother."

"This is Erabesque," Ingamald fought to control her embarrassment, "sister to the Troubadour, mistress of dance and who knows what else."

"Indeed who?" laughed the dark woman. She pulled Ingamald to her in an affectionate embrace, kissing the blush on both her cheeks. "And this?" She turned her smouldering gaze to Lira, who introduced herself timidly. "Well. So." Erabesque sniffed the air. "Is there food?"

"There is stew brewing for this evening's supper. Until then an apple will have to do. I know you care little for porridge."

Erabesque was already at the cauldron tasting its contents. "Ah, witch. You know nothing of spice." She produced a small pouch from the layers of silk at her waist and added more than a pinch to the bubbling brew.

"Erabesque! Not everyone appreciates yours!"

"Fools they then!"

Ingamald laughed and stole back the spoon from her guest, adding wryly, "I see the sun pleases you not. It sets within the hour."

Erabesque yawned and shrugged. "Like the cat and the owl, I prefer the stars."

Lira, speechless, watched the dark woman stroll restlessly about the cottage. "Where are the others? Did you get the girl? What is her secret? When do we sup?" Erabesque's questions, answered calmly by Ingamald, left the Learned woman dizzy.

"And you? Lira, it is? What is your crime?"

"I read."

"Ah."

"And teach others to read."

"It is enough. For him. The Winter. He is fearful of knowledge. He forbids it. He is terrified of those who know. Lest they depose him, dispose of him."

"How is one to do that?" Ingamald bid Erabesque take a chair and sat opposite, next to Lira.

"How? It is the question on everyone's lips. Maghenta, my mother's. My brother's. Yours. Those in peril. Those who raise the voice of dissention. How?"

"Your mother, she is well?"

Erabesque frowned. "Not so well... since this trouble began. It drains her. This trouble. Brooding on it does her ill."

Ingamald nodded, understanding Erabesque's disquiet. The Musica woman would lead her people as matriarch should Maghenta turn too sick or worse. Erabesque faced an onerous responsibility, especially in these times so fraught with danger.

"Aye. So it is with Hana. She is well, but sleeps fitfully, mindful always of what the future bodes. Like me, she has consulted the stars, cast the runes, but we can find no solutions...only visions of a darkling time."

"Ah yes. There is likewise a darkness, a blackness in the cards. I consult the Fortuna often, but their message is the same. The Fool keeps turning up, and in reverse."

The air was stilled in Nookeshea, punctuated only by bubbling of the stew.

Erabesque clapped her hands sharply. "Away with these thoughts. Tonight we have each other and in each other lies the answer, no?"

"Aye!" Ingamald rose and smiled through the window at the party of gatherers new returned and laden with kindling and water. She looked fondly at the Troubadour jesting with Yda, who seemed to have warmed considerably to the Musica man. A spasm chilled her witch's spine. There would be mirth tonight, but of days to come she could not be certain.

Yda sat wide-eyed before the merry party. She sipped at the redolent liquid in her cup. Roccoco, the Troubadour had called it. It made her throat burn a little; the flavour was like a sweet and not like. Before her, the three women danced, but no such as she had seen before. Yda was used to jigs and turns, and Lira seemed also familiar with these. But the black-haired and the copper-haired danced as though maddened. The child wondered silently if this dancing were for good or ill.

Ingamald pulled the girl to her feet and bade her join them. Yda looked at each of the adults. The Troubadour flashed golden at her over the neck of his zantauri; she tenuously tapped her feet. Capo played his instrument with eyes closed, his face rapt and awash with perspiration. Yda allowed herself to sway. Erabesque's eyes were smoke-filled, entranced. The child began to twirl. Lira smiled at her revolutions with delight and encouragement, and she, too, began to circle the room. But Ingamald's face was dazzling, aflame, her hair crackling with sparks of light matching that in her eyes. The witchy woman moved with abandon, thrusting her torso here, her neck there. Arms raised above her head as if beckoning passion into them. Hips in intricate gyration. If Yda had not herself been now so swept up in the music, spicy as their evening repast, she might have been afraid.

Just when she could twirl no longer, the music stopped. Panting dancers collapsed in chairs or simply on the floor. The Troubadour and his Musica fellow wiped the sweat from their respective zantauris and replaced them lovingly in their cases. Heartbeats slowed; the fire was stoked; cups of roccoco drained. Beezle slinked from shadowy somewhere into Ingamald's lap.

Talk began softly, turning grave. Yda's head dropped to her chest.

A sudden blare of light shocked her alert. She was first to reach the cottage window. The others joined her, peering out to the darkness. And then another pinpoint burst of coloured light soared off into the sky, erupting into a thousand dazzling points of green. Still another soared immediately after, bursting into purple burning stars. An audible awe filled the cottage.

"Ingo!" Ingamald's excited voice was at the door. She threw it open and ran out into the chill night air. Within a moment the witch dragged a new stranger into the midst of Nookeshea.

"My friend, fire-eater Ingo!"

Ingamald beamed at her motley companion. An adept at fire-tossing, juggling and tumbling, Ingo could indeed swallow flame. The young wiccan woman had seen him do so many times in the market of Ruheplatz. In addition to his fiery sports, Ingo was also reputedly lock-pick, coxy cutpurse and general scallywag. A welcome and jocose troublemaker to assist with their seditious plotting.

Introductions and welcome made, a bowl of stew thrust into Ingo's hands, chairs pulled nearer round in a tighter circle, and the fire-mage told his tale. Yda gawked at this latest addition; the Troubadour scowled; Lira wondered.

"So the proclimition was berned to bits, by the loiks o' me, an 'umble performer."

"What did it say, Ingo?"

"Dunno. You're the one 'at can read, witch. Never learned me letters."

"It is the same proclamation posted on the gates or walls of every city, town and village in Hinterlünd. It says what we all have most feared of the tyrant." Lira recited from memory, "'First: Be ye advised that all forms of magick are hereby expressly forbidden unless commissioned by Lord Morton Cornelius Winter, at his bidding, for his pleasure or entertainment solely. Persons discovered independently practicing or investigating magick or any arcane art will be punished. Repeat offenders will be put to death.

"'Second: Be ye advised that midwives and healers, practitioners of the Craft are hereafter outlawed. Any woman or girl discovered practicing these arts will be punished. Repeat offenders will be put to death.

"'Third: Be ye advised that vagabonds and itinerant rovers—including those who fall within the categories of the Rowan or Musica—are hereafter ordered to assign themselves to profitable labour. These persons will be barred from Sprïggen and Ruheplatz after the midnight hour. Trespassers and poachers on lands under Lord Morton Cornelius Winter's watch will be dealt with severely.

"'Fourth: Be ye advised that hereafter the study of letters and words, the reading and writing of books is from this time banned. Persons known as Learneds are heretofore forbidden to sell or trade in books. Those who persist will be imprisoned and punished. Those who seek out the services of the Learneds will likewise be punished.

"'Fifth: Be ye advised that all persons who are physically unfit for profitable labour—those crippled, maimed or defective in some manner—are banished from Hinterlünd by order of Lord Morton Cornelius Winter. Persons with such infirmities are hereby ordered to report to the Court of Sprïggen for assessment. Those discovered at large will be put to death.

"'Sixth: Be ye advised that all forms of festival, music, dance and entertainment require a signed permit and tithe payment. Permits will be obtained from officials of the court of Lord Morton Cornelius Winter only after Lord Winter has assessed the appropriateness of the proffered festival or performance. Musicians, jugglers, artists and other performers are subject to official investigation and cannot perform without signed permit and tithe payment. These persons will be barred from Sprïggen and Ruheplatz after the midnight hour. Violators will be punished.

"'Seventh: Be ye advised that every citizen of Hinterlünd is hereby required to pay tax on up to but not exceeding three-quarters of annual earnings, crops, livestock or income. No person is exempt. Violators will face severe penalties.'"

Faces around the circle were sombre or sullen. Moments passed.

A low chuckle rumbled in the witch's throat. It grew to a chortle. A guffaw. Ingamald laughed out loud. Freely. Others looked quizzical. The Troubadour smiled. Then she laughed again. And again. Until slowly, her amusement spread through the room. Hearty witchy laughter, joined with her friends', regaled the rafters. Even Beezle meowed in merriment.

Wiping tears from her face, she sputtered, "What a fine band of reprobates have I here in Nookeshea! A dangerous gaggle of felons! A juggler, a woman, a child, a dancer and two musicians! I fear for my very life!"

Laughter still rang in the room when next she spoke. “See how much power we truly have, friends. What a fearful and puny man is this Winter. How sure his insecurity.

“What needs doing is to keep doing. Thus to work Winter’s undoing. We need a map.” A broad arch of her hand materialized a map of Hinterlünd on the floor within the circle. Illuminated, sites on the map sparkled as Ingamald recited placenames. “Mirt for the Musica. Ut for Ingo. Lira and Yda to Leiben. I will to Ruheplatz, then to Mountain Vale.

“In each we find, we free. After a fortnight, we meet in Nookeshea, safe in this circle within Bruë Wood. To find havens for the liberated. Then to plot another course, set out again. Consider how to reach the man through subterfuge. What think you all?”

“Aye!”

“Yes!”

“So!”

The edges of the map were dissolving. “Then tonight we to bed. Our tomorrows to task!” Ingamald’s eyes radiated confidence.

She allowed Lira and Yda to settle in the cottage as she stepped out to bid the others good night, Ingo adopting Lira’s former sleeping caravan. Ingamald walked to the darkest edge of the stone circle.

“Ah. The witch is restless.”

Ingamald felt pleasure at the voice near her ear. “Perchance.”

“You were dazzling tonight.”

“Aye?”

“Spellbinding.” He touched her hair. “Though I care little for the man.”

“Morton Winter?”

“No, Ingamald. You know who I mean.”

She turned her face to him. “Ingo is harmless, Troubadour.”

“Even so?” His lips grazed hers.

“Aye.”

He wrapped her hair about his hand. “You are a woman not easily tamed.”

“How long have you known this?”

“Morton Winter would be wise to keep well away from this one. He is no match for her.” The Troubadour touched his lips to her nape.

Let us hope, she thought silently. Let us hope.

CHAPTER

INGAMALD ROSE EARLY. Careful not to wake the others, she stole from the cottage, two large baskets in hand. Behind her fluttering cloak padded Beezle. In the pre-dawn darkness her feet sensed the way. She stepped beyond the stone circle into Bruë Wood and towards the brook. Once there she bathed, skyclad, in the frigid waters. Cloaked anew, she began to wander near the banks, searching and humming, as Beezle moused nearby. Clever witch hands sought out the last of autumn's bounty: sweet scented grasses, edible fern fiddleheads and mushrooms, late fall berries and nuts. Dawn chirpings accompanied her ancient melody; her feet crunched dead leaves on the forest floor. Adding at the last some pine cones and fir branches, she stood up to stretch from her crouch and saw him.

In between the tree trunks, almost their very colour, a beautiful young man dressed in hide and feather. But ten paces away, he was very still, and Ingamald felt that he had been watching her for the entire hour of her gathering.

"It is you." She smiled into his eyes. When he said nothing, she continued. "I have much to thank you for. I am no hunter, so meat and fish are a luxury."

He nodded once.

"I hope your hurt has healed."

Again he nodded.

"I would have done more for you that day. But I see how you prefer to keep your own company."

Ingamald sat on a boulder and placed her baskets, one empty, one full, near her feet. "Now winter draws nigh, and I have been worried for you. Most certainly you can fend for yourself in these woods. But snow and sleet are cheerless companions. Where are your people?"

The young man said nothing but stepped forward from the trees. He padded silently to the wicca woman who rose to greet him. With his approach she caught a fragrance, sweet and smoky. He stood facing her, and his beauty made her stammer.

"I- I am called Ingamald."

He nodded, staring at her eyes. Her hair.

"Today is All Sprites' Eve. It is a special day, a sacred day for... for me. For witches. I am a witch. Today I gather for this evening's feast. A celebration. We honour and welcome the change in the world."

Still he stared into her flushing face.

"Wh- what are you called?"

Ingamald waited. Whimsically, the wind blew up, flipping back the hood of her cape to reveal her hair, a wild-tossed copper in the dawn light. A jay called. Its mate answered. The wind settled.

The young man spoke at last. "Roc." And he touched his black braid with one hand and her sunlit hair with his other.

With that touch, Ingamald felt. The story of his loss. Of the Rowan people, in particular Roc's family. She saw the burning time. A night attack. The slaughter of the innocent and defenceless as they slept. His tormented escape, tormented because he could do nothing but escape. The pain of his wounds, those that healed, those that would never.

When he released her hair, she was sorry. She longed to weave hers with his for healing, for life. Instead, she simply sighed. "I thank you for your story. Though it is very harsh, I am honoured that you trust me."

"Yes." Roc's voice echoed the rustling leaves.

"You are welcome to our feast this eve. You are welcome in my home. Roc."

He shook his head.

"You are most welcome!"

"The people."

"My friends are your friends. I see behind your tale the spectre of the very man we seek to undo. He has a name, Roc. The menace that destroyed your family, your happiness. He is Winter, Morton Winter."

She watched his face. He kept it very still. "And we work to release those in the tyrant's clutches. So my friends would bid you welcome, as have I."

"Morton Winter." An icy blast swept them by.

"Aye. A cold name befitting a cold man." She paused, looked into Roc's dark eyes. "Come you then, this eve?"

He backed surely away from her, his retreat silent as his approach. He seemed to melt into the trees.

"Roc?" Ingamald's voice was sharp.

"Ingamald." His came from somewhere already deeper into Bruë Wood.

Shaking herself from the spell of this encounter, Ingamald took the first basketload back to Nookeshea, then trudged the footpath towards Wellhørst village market to buy apples, a pumpkin and sundry staples for All Sprites' Eve feast. Several coins secreted in her cloak by the Troubadour clinked cheerfully as she walked. But Ingamald's thoughts were not with the Troubadour.

When she returned, the guests were busy about. Lira and Yda were sweeping the cobwebs out of Nookeshea. Together they cleaned the hearth and emptied her ashes. The Troubadour had gathered bracken and dead branches, and now chopped wood. Water waited in several buckets; Ingo fetched more as they emptied through the day. Capo erected a spit and fire far enough away from the Musica caravans.

"Ingamald, look what the sprites have given us!" Erasbeque's musical voice bellowed out through the trees as she danced from the brook. In one hand she carried four newly skinned hares; in the other, their pelts. Never squeamish, she had cleaned and prepared the animals for the feast.

"There are no sprites roaming until tonight, Erabesque. These are gifts from a man."

The Musica woman raised an eyebrow. "So?"

"Aye. A Rowan man who lives in Bruë Wood. A friend."

Ingamald tossed her hair and left Erabesque musing, as Capo skewered the game over the fire.

Inside Nookeshea, Ingamald set to work whisking eggs, milk and flour. She gutted the pumpkin, adding its pulp to the mixture. Outside, the Learned woman and her six and six fingered helper lit a fire in the small stone oven. By the time the witch brought out the pans brimming with fragrant batter, the oven was piping hot. She paused to admire Ingo's carving of the jack o'lantern.

"'Ere's a jack o' nape, Ingamald! What think ye o' the loiks o' 'im?"

"Aye, he's a jack, if e'er I saw any. And I think he bears the likes of you, Ingo!"

"Ha! Ye are a witch!"

"And glad am I that you have noticed!" She laughed merrily and ducked from the piece of pumpkin rind Ingo flung at her in jest.

Apples bobbed, ripe and red, in a large tub of water. The hares, cooked and golden, nestled on a bed of ferns and fiddleheads. Several cakes sat cooling on the table beside them. Nuts awaited cracking in a nearby bowl. Fragrant pine decorated the still-cold hearth and the door to Nookeshea. A candle flickered taunts behind the mad gaze of Jack, the pumpkin in the window.

Outdoors in the stone circle, each member of the party had gathered and marked a stone with his or her name. With these, they constructed a smaller circle to enclose the now-flaming bonfire. Its heat cast a reddish glow over the celebrants. Ingo lit six smaller blazes at intervals about the greater stone circle around Nookeshea.

"Hark!" Ingamald, with Beezle poised on her left shoulder, raised her arms above her hands to the stars. "It is the night of sprites. We welcome the good; expel the bad. We give thanks for this feast of autumn's plenty, open our arms to the coming winter, wax strong and certain that we will survive, know that without winter, there can be no spring."

The party sobered at her resonant voice.

"Tonight is for revelry and ha'e-madness. Tonight is for tomfoolery and mayhem. Tonight we expose our senses to the other worlds. A gate closes; another opens. No one of us knows how or why. It is a wonder.

"We place this chalice, an offering, beyond the edge of the circle. We place the chalice to both honour and avert the sprites who journey this eve from their place in otherworlds."

She nodded to Yda who grasped the pewter chalice firmly in twelve fingers. The child raised the cup to Lira. She filled it with a concoction Ingamald bottled and preserved in the root cellar beneath Nookeshea. Yda then marched solemnly to the edge of the stone circle and placed the chalice beyond its security. The child moved briskly back to the witch's side.

"And now!" Ingamald pronounced carefully, "Let the Eve of Sprites' spree commence!" Beezle leaped from her shoulders at the wiccan signal, darting in and out and between legs and skirts in ecstatic cat-frenzy.

Ingamald lit a torch from the great bonfire; each of her fellows did the same. A company of songsters circled widdershins about the great flame, torches raised high.

On All Sprites' Eve
All griefs take leave
So give us leave
To begin anew

On All Sprites' Eve
We beg reprieve
From foul or ill
The Reaper's chill

Come out, come out
We beckon ye
We reckon ye
Are drawing nigh
Avert all malice
Ill fortune
Drink from the chalice
Accept our boon

On All Sprites' Eve
Do not deceive
With trick or spell
Ye can conceive
On All Sprites' Eve
'Fore light of day
Depart in peace
And go your way

On All Sprites' Eve
All griefs take leave
So give us leave
To begin anew
On All Sprites' Eve

As the last strain faded, Ingamald led the others into Nookeshea and placed her torch in the barren hearth. The others did likewise. Ingo added more logs until until a hearty fire blazed. The meat was carved; the feasting began.

In their pieces of pumpkin cake, the Troubadour and Yda found coins, signifying wealth to come. Lira found the brass ring Ingamald had planted, foretelling a second marriage. The witch's portion contained the thimble, and the Troubadour frowned at this portent that Ingamald would never marry. She, herself, laughed and dared him to find the apple with the coin. He bobbed foolishly away, taking turns with Ingo, Lira and Yda, and in the end, it was indeed the Musica man who won the prize.

Each quarter hour, the fire-eater left the cottage to feed the fires burning through All Sprites' night.

Between cracking nuts, Erabesque read the Fortuna for any who wished to consult the cards. Ingo learned that he would narrowly escape a severe burning and was warned that he would be smitten with a comely wench within the year. Yda dreamed of the pretty frocks the Fortuna promised. In good humour, she straightened the crook of Capo's walking stick, and coaxed it back once more to his relief and to much applause.

Ingamald told a hair-raising tale about the ghost of Gestford Copse, far to the east. Near the midnight hour, the revellers dashed out to the bonfire. They adorned themselves with masks made of woven grasses or simply smeared soot onto their faces. Ingo pulled out a theatrical mask from his collection, Ingamald a feathered creation of her own making. So masked, they danced about the fire to the music of the zantauris, and that of their own laughter and making. No one noticed the dancer in hide and feather who joined them from the shadows and disappeared as quickly when the music ceased. No one but Ingamald who watched satisfied as he discovered the small bundle of food at the base of the nearest fir tree.

Just moments before midnight, she shooed the party into

Nookeshea and bolted the solid door. More wood was piled on the hearthfire. Faces were washed; masks burned. People settled into nooks and corners, or reclined on the reed mat floor, secure in the warmth of the place and each other. Yda leaned against Lira. Erabesque claimed the rocking chair. Ingamald rested her head on the Troubadour's lap, his hand caught in the tangle of her tresses.

And the voices came. Softly, breezily at first. Then more and more urgent. Knocking the shutters of the cottage. Whistling about the thatched roof. Growing insistent, mocking. Speaking in many tongues, all tongues. Shrieking regret. Talking torment. Begging trespass. The company, wide-eyed and watchful, listened intently. Ingo added more wood to the fire, settled back on his haunches. No one spoke. A banging sounded on the door. No one rose to answer. Hours dripped by. Voices ebbed and flowed. Swept up wildly. Sighed downwards. Eventually away. Exhausted, the vigilants slept. Except Ingamald.

At dawn, with her cloak secure about her shoulders, she quitted Nookeshea to greet the first day of the new year. Raising her arms, she embraced the sun. A walk to the edge of the stone circle revealed that the chalice had been dumped, emptied of its contents. Pieces of thatching were flung into the circle, but the roof could be easily mended. The pine boughs over the door were gone, carried off by some cacophonous blast.

She counted the rocks of the bonfire. Where there were nine, now there were but eight. Alarmed, she counted again. There was the Troubadour's name, Erasbeque, Lira, Yda, Ingo and Capo—written for them in Yda's childish script—one for Ingamald, one stone for the great mother. Then whose? Which stone was taken? Ingamald froze.

"Happy new year, witch of my heart." The Troubadour's voice was warm at her ear. She turned stiffly and he kissed her, pulling back to look at her sharply. "So? What ails Ingamald?"

"Hana! Hana is gone!"

"What say you?"

"Her stone, Troubadour! Her stone! That I placed for her. Last e'en were nine rocks. This morn only eight. Hana is gone!"

"I scarce understand these your customs. I little knew what all we did last eve. Explain to me. This missing stone. Hana?"

"See you not? It means..." Ingamald struggled to control her tears, "A stone gone missing during All Sprites' Eve portends death to the name writ thereon. Hana! Troubadour, Hana will die this year!"

"Nay, Ingamald, nay." The Musica man held the witch, love and friend, as closely as he could. "Nay. It will not come to pass."

Somewhere in the nearby trees an owl hooted and the Troubadour started.

"Ohhh, Morrrrrtooon!" whined an eager voice.

"Ooooh, Corneeeelius!" wheezed an ecstatic second.

"Eeeeee, Winnnnnter!" panted a fervent third.

"What, you fiends? I am sleeping, idiots!"

"We know, Morrrrrtooon!" teased the voice.

"Yessssss, Corneeeeliusssssssss! We've found her!" hissed the second.

"Ahhhh, Winnnnnter! The one who crosses you, the magic one," the third dangled.

"What?" Morton Winter sat upright in bed.

"We know, Morrrrrtooon!"

"We know where, Corneeeelius"

"But we cannot tell, Winnnnnter!"

Winter swiped at the air with his fist. "What means this? Why torment me with your knowing! Tell me all!!!"

"We are bound by the laws of magic, Morrrrrtooooon," sobbed the first voice.

"A stone circle forbids us, Corneeeelius!" the second jeered.

"But we can give you one piece of knowledge, one you will cherish. Another's name, Winnnnnter!" promised the third.

"Give it me, give it me!" Morton Winter sprinted from his bed, demanding wisdom from the air.

"Asssssk, nicccccеely, Morrrrrtttoooon!"

"Mind your manners, Corneeeeeliusss!"

"Remember your messengers, Winnnnnnter!"

"All right, all right. There will be some extra morsel for you on the window sills this very evening!"

Sibilant laughter hissed about the cold chamber.

"Some careless, beyond the stone circle, tripped! So we could take a stone."

"Some clumsy, in a hurry through the wood, spilled the contents! But we could only steal one stone."

"Some clod, unknowing of his folly, tipped over the chalice! So we chose carefully this stone."

"Cretins! You speak in riddles! Speak clearly or leave me!" Moron choked on his impatience.

"We give you a name, Morrrrrtoon!"

"We give you a witch, Corneeeeeliussss!

All three voices rose in jubilant, malicious chorus. "Hana of Hören Wood!"

CHAPTER

THE DWARF PUT ONE THICK FOOT in front of the other. Again and again. Snow crunched beneath his weight. Chill November air smarted his cheeks and forehead, what remained uncovered. His own cold breathing silvered his yellow beard and mustache.

He willed away fatigue. Willed away memories. Thoughts. But still they came. Of his wife, Midred. Dead six month and two year. Plague or poison. It mattered not now. Winter had him in his cold clutches. Just as he had long sought to do. For four year and more. Tried to win the dwarf with wheedling. Flattery. Then threats. To do his bidding. Leave hearth and smithy and good, honest work. Work making fine things. Strong things. Useful things. As in the tradition of his people. Iron. Bronze. Silver. Gold. Things with wise purpose or simple beauty. To leave family and work for Winter. Making wicked things. Ugly things. Destructive things. Turning all—iron, bronze, silver, gold—to leaden weight.

Dagnott paused under a fir tree. Opened his pouch and withdrew the dried meat made by the Rowan woman for this travel. He chewed, swallowed, did not taste. All was tasteless to him now. Now that Winter's chill grip held him fast.

And after Midred died, the boy…left. Gone. Lost. Wenceslas. Their only child. Only just walking. One night vanished from the sturdy crib Dagnott, himself, had fashioned. Waking, the father stared at the tousled coverlet made by Midred's hand. Empty. A stolen child. A changling, some whispered. How sad. Pity. He could not stand the villagers pity.

He looked. Everywhere. Wore himself out with looking. Asking. Faery folk swore they did not snatch the boy. The village wise woman lacked the wisdom to know Wenceslas's whereabouts. Rowan people—any he could discover or coax from their hiding in the trees—knew naught. No word. No one knew. No one saw or had seen. And so passed a summer of tears, a fall of frowns. And finally Winter.

Dagnott turned to Winter who had, they said, a remarkable thing of no man's making. A black table that told all. The truth. The truth, if one dared face it. Dagnott would know the truth. He would look on this table.

But not so. Not at first. First there were favours for the frosty tyrant. Dagnott's first construction was shackles. His clever mind and hands for designing had never been put to such use. Dagnott despised his new work. Chains and bars for prison cells. All manner of stocks. Iron cages. Iron masks. Spikes. Instruments for treatments he dared not think of—they gave him night terrors. Sweating and toiling over the smithy fires, the dwarf worked for a year. Often asked to see the master. To ask after the boy. If Dagnott did enough work, Master Winter would grant him audience with the table, and the dwarf would ask and know. What to be—if the boy were alive—then joyous and hopefilled. Or if Wenceslas was dead, then Dagnott could die, too.

Waiting furrowed his brow. Work bent his back. Hours of toil gnarled his fingers. Dagnott cared not. For anything. Anyone. He only cared to know.

At last he spoke with Winter. Late summer.

"I have laboured long, Master Winter."

"Ah, yes. And we have provided well for you, man. Food. A bed. Ale. Wenches, if ever you willed. An excellent smithy equipped with solid tools. What more could a dwarf wish?"

Dagnott ignored the slight. He knew Winter bore his race ill will, saw them as deficient both in size and intelligence. Good only for slavery and hard labour. He had heard of the persecutions, but so intent at his purpose, had chosen to ignore and work heedlessly on. Again, he swallowed his pride.

"Lord, I would know about my boy. Wenceslas. I would know if he lives…"

"Or rots."

The dwarf cast down his eyes. "Aye."

"I see. And think you that I have the answer?"

"Aye, Lord, I do. You have the black table." Still Dagnott watched the ground.

"Ah, Tabula. My Tabula." Winter's voice was a cold caress. "You wish to consult her?"

"Aye."

"Never!"

Dagnott felt a fiery furnace blast into being deep within. This time he looked to the white spectre of a man before him. So frail. One crack of Dagnott's hammer. A twist of that thin white neck in a thick dwarfish hand. But Morton Winter's next words beat down the fire smouldering within the dwarf.

"But! I will ask on your behalf." His words were cool. Slippery. But Winter did ask. The dwarf watched his white highness float to the black table. Unveil it and look deep into its face. Winter asked the stone slab many questions about Wenceslas. His words, his way, seemed sincere. But when he returned to the dais and the dwarf, Winter's words were brusque.

"Tabula told me naught. She is willful. But she knows something! I saw knowledge flash across her face. I will try again, on your behalf. Only…," Morton Winter licked his bluish lips, "work well for me, my dwarf."

"Aye, Lord Winter. As always, I do your bidding." And as Dagnott stepped from the antechamber, Winter's fist about his throat nearly suffocated him.

But work Dagnott had done and did. Well-wrought things at Winter's command and for his command. Sometimes things of silver—which Winter liked well and for his own pleasure or entertainment. Dagnott toiled on, closing his ears to the ugly whispers about him, about the plight of his people, the plight of others. While he worked, he kept silent. Only speaking orders to the few attendants and workers. Only keeping one thought in his head: Wenceslas, his boy. His last, lost love.

And Winter had asked the Tabula again. Thrice. Each time at the dwarf's request. After a sufficient period of work. After a particularly difficult piece was finished. After a fine piece crafted for the master's personal adornment. At each asking, the Tabula revealed traces of knowing, but remained mute. And each time, Morton Winter promised to ask again.

So a thin promise was Dagnott's only hope. And as he plunged through the falling, thickening late November snow, his heart cried out silently in the dark for the lost boy.

Ahead the lights of a town flickered dimly. Mountain Vale. There would be an inn. Grog. Ale. And mayhaps some news about the stolen prisoners. Stolen like Wenceslas. Dagnott would find the thieves or their whereabouts and upon his return to Sprïggen, the Tabula would tell about those other thieves who had stolen his treasure.

He trudged upwards, towards the weak light.

Morton Winter loosened his sash, adjusted the folds of his silver robe.

"Morrrrrton!" breezed the first voice, "Are you well?"

"Corneeelius!" hissed the second, "You look a little swollen!"

"Winnnnter!" nayed the third, "Is that a potted belly you try to hide?"

"Silence, you chattering sprites! Have you nothing better to do or say? I have already one fool, and he is fool enough!"

Their taunts told true. Winter had grown a substantial paunch of late; the tailors were busy altering his clothes. A white frown fixed his face.

"Tabula, darling! Relieve me of these babbling idlers. Show me something. I wish to know."

Having already stripped away her silver wrapping, Morton gazed into the black face of his mute beloved and saw:

Out and beyond the castle walls. Over the moat and up the crest of an ancient hill where rests a stone hut. Through the crude door. Into a dimly candlelit chamber of the alchemist.

Glint of glass and vial and bottle. Bubbling concoctions over a minor flame. Glass bulbs distilling and brewing liquids of various hues: violet, amber, cloudy white. Copper apparatus. Measuring instruments. Scales and weights. A bar of pure gold. A bar of pure silver.

A bespectacled bent figure works at his bench. His face, slightly averted, is cast in a shadow of concentration. Morton Winter has never met the man, this alchemist in his employ these three years. Keeps to himself. Never leaves the stone hut. Supplies are brought to and left at the door. Only this man is allowed the hated books for his occupation. And any other tomes he may request. All is granted him. For it is no simple task, this quest. He works solidly on the elixir Morton Winter craves. Morton Winter who wills to freeze life. His own. And thus to keep ever alive. The alchemist raises a glass tube to the candlelight, shakes it once, twice. Replaces it in the clamp and lights another flame beneath. He turns his back as the vision fades.

To a mean tiny room in the castle proper. There is no heat in the cold cell, and a misshapen creature shivers beneath a thin, ratty blanket on the shelf that serves for bed. Didion slumbers on instead of rousing to his labours. Morton Winter silently notes that a sharp reprimand is owing. The scene of the sleeping hunchback dissolves.

And finds a dwarf panting up a rocky incline towards a tiny hamlet, Mountain Vale. Snow is swirling about his boots. An unkind wind threatens to remove the traveller's humble cloak, and he draws the hood tightly over his head.

He stumbles into the village, pausing at the well. There is no inn in the place. And so the stunted figure travels from door to door, seeking shelter from the elements. All are slammed shut. Until he reaches a last cottage, away from the main street, behind a small cluster of houses.

A sturdy young woman smiles through the doorway. Throwing on a shawl, she leads the dwarf to a rickety shed in the back of her dwelling. Together they enter, and Dagnott collapses on the straw bed she has provided him.

Instantly the scene moves back to a room high in the north tower of Morton Winter's castle. Therein a too-small boy sits on a woven mat, amusing himself with two wooden spoons. A woman rocks nearby, darning small woolen socks. There is a scant fire in the grate of the huge fireplace. Wenceslas asks his guardian a soundless question. She shakes her head, and he turns a stricken face back to his wooden friends.

A swirl of colour, and the trees of Hören Wood appear. Rough-hewn men tramp through the forest. Searching. For a sign. A hut. They pause, puzzled. For they know these woods well. And silver is promised them. But they are lost in these woods bewitched. Winter mumbles his discontent.

So that Tabula now turns her attention to an easterly town Morton does not recognize. A diminutive woman is aside a covered cart, its doors flung open to the market square. She hands out books to the citizens with her right hand, while with her left, holds open a text she reads to a small group of children seated at her feet.

"Thieves! Magicians! Witches! Learneds! I will rout these out and whip them to butter!"

Furious, Morton Winter slammed his fist upon the obsidian table. Tabula's face turned abruptly blank. He abandoned her and stormed to the silver cord at his barren bedside. There was naught else to do this evening. Within moments, a bevy of servants entered his quarters.

"Send for the poison taster and some of the roast piglet from last night's supper!"

CHAPTER

"MASTER, THE PEOPLE WILL NOT HEAR OF IT!"

"They will do my bidding or feel my sting, Didion." Winter's breath in the hunchback's face was stale and chill.

"Villagers and peasants will revolt." Didion shook his head.

The man in motley next the dais, leapt up. "The peasants are revolting! Hideous, in fact."

"Silence, you scurvy scapegrace! When I have need of a fool, I'll ask for one."

"What fool needs a fool?" Tiny bells on the foolscap jangled.

"I said silence!" Morton Winter turned his irritation back to Didion. "It isn't insult enough that I must endure this cursed Yule season. Carnival is salt in my wounds. How many weeks until this blasted festival, say you?"

"Shy of a dozen, Master."

Winter looked about his great chamber. He had forbidden any Yuletide decorations, despising them and the silly carols the people insisted on singing. Still, he could sense the advantage of these repugnant celebrations. Merrymaking kept the masses malleable because happy idiots made ignorant idiots. Yes, there was a certain pleasure in that knowledge. If power meant putting on a show every twelve or so weeks to keep the churls compliant, then so be it. Morton Winter settled back into his great silver throne. He lifted his lip in a smirk.

"I 'gin to see your point, Didion. You are not as stupid as you appear. I will permit the Carnival. In fact, I heartily endorse it. Make it known, Didion, put up a proclamation."

"Another, Master?"

"Another, Didion."

"So many proclamations, Lord Winter. So many illiterates, as per your decree. Soon there will be fewer and fewer who can read your notices."

"Just as I wish. So send the town criers forth, as well."

"Aye, my lord." The misshapen form turned to go, but paused, downcast. "Master Winter, there is one favour I would beg. I, too, am fond of Yule celebrations. I beg your leave to leave the castle, to sojourn briefly in my village."

"The very village that reviled and hated you?"

"Aye, my lord. I would go under cover of darkness." The hunchback looked at his hands. "My father grows frail."

Morton Winter selected another of the Yuletide treats, the only thing in this blasted season that sweetened his sour mood. He readjusted his growing girth on the cushion of his throne, and passed silently a bit of foul wind.

"The only time, Didion, my grotesque friend," Winter's words were muffled with chewing, "that you will quit this castle is when I banish you to that wretched bell tower from whence I rescued you. Happy Yule. Leave my sight."

Didion left as he was bid and wandered lonely through the cold corridors. His clumsy feet stumbled down flights of steps. He kept to the shadows, as always, avoiding the pretty servants, the men in livery. All found him repulsive. All save one. He wound his way down to the dungeons and pushed the secret stone. The wall scraped open, revealing the passage beneath the castle. Only two persons knew about the stone and this corridor. Grasping a torch ensconced in the wall, Didion traversed the musty, damp tunnel towards his one place of refuge. He knocked at the trap door. It swung open. A fool reached a hand to help the hunchback.

The dwarf, travel-weary and haggard, limped to the dais. He stood waiting before the rogue lord.

"Well, Dagnott. You have been long gone."

"I fell ill, Master Winter."

Morton Winter said nothing. The quiet was punctuated by the cracking of nuts. He popped the sweetmeats into his mouth, dropped the shells on the floor a servant, with brush and dustpan, promptly swept clean.

"I found them not, Master."

The pale, bethroned man picked at his teeth with a sharp blue fingernail.

"I learned little." The dwarf coughed, a dry hacking. "But I know who the thieves are."

"Indeed? Tell me, dwarf."

"A group of vigilantes. Misfits, outcasts, vagabonds. One is some kind of juggler or japester. Their place of hiding is impossible to find. Bound as it is under some magic spell of protection."

"And their leader? Who is he?"

"She is a witch."

"Ha! Hana of Hören Wood!"

"No, Master."

"Then who?" Winter's eyes were glinting crystals. He leaned forward, hungrily.

Dagnott paused. He thought of the cold night he fell very ill and of a young woman who'd cheered and warmed him. Welcomed him to her home. Nursed him well again. Guileless. Kind. Her children and silent husband likewise. Dagnott lay sick for weeks, and she attended him. Sall. Good, honest Sall. Who shared with him vittles and stories. Touched him. So that he felt again warmth and human compassion. She told him the tale of her friends.

"Do not try my patience, dwarf! Have you forgotten your purpose and your son?"

Dagnott stared at the loathsome creature before him, grown soft and round, if not paler with the weeks. He considered Sall again. Her sympathy for his losses, his missing son. Her amiable chatter as she applied salve to his frostbitten ears. And shared words about her closest friend.

Morton's serpent words struck at Dagnott's thoughts. "Tabula gave me a glimpse of Wenceslas's whereabouts."

The dwarf's eyes misted. He drew a single, miserable breath. "Ingamald. The witch you seek is called Ingamald."

"Good Yuletidings, friend Didion." The fool embraced the hunchback fondly.

"Aye, and also to you. If any tidings these sorry days be good."

"Ah, my friend," the fool removed his cap, began to unfasten his motley costume. "You are in a glum mood. Here, this will cheer you." The host poured his guest a goblet of spiced wine, warmed in a decanter over a flame on a cluttered worktable.

Didion emptied the goblet as his friend donned spectacles and a warmer robe, black and velvet, then lit a peat fire in the stove grate.

"Ah, Fool," Didion spoke warmly lifting his cup in salute, "You are indeed an alchemist!"

"And you, Hunchback, are a Learned man!" They laughed and refilled their cups. "Here, another book for you. A fine specimen. A history."

Didion received the gift humbly. Fingered the leathern cover, the gold letters. Opened the cover and lost himself within the illustrated parchment pages. Sighing, closed the text and thanked his companion. "What would I be without words, Svalbaard?"

"A lesser man, Didion. We, both of us, would be lesser men."

Ingamald wove before a late-evening fire. A Yule log burned and a small fir tree, festooned with dried fruits and popped corn, stood fragrantly nearby. Lira and Yda slept. In Ingamald's own bed, Hana dreamed safe. A winter storm battled outside. The witch pulled her cloak closer about her shoulders and looked to her only waking companion. Beezle luxuriated before her on the hearthrug, flipping his black tail.

"Beezle cat, I will finish these before the morrow, or fall asleep trying." Doggedly, her needle pierced onwards. Beside her lay a completed tapestry, small but sufficient for a pillow slip. It featured a book open to an illustrated scene of lively dancing folk around a bonfire. The piece she now worked on was a picture of two hands, each delicate and six-fingered, holding another book, closed and bearing the simple title, "Yda". The witch sighed. She had had little time for weaving.

In the weeks since All Sprites' Eve, she and the others had been a'busy at subterfuge. Guile and disguise. Skulk and stealth. Filching sneakthievery. Ingamald chuckled above her needle.

By the Nones of November, the company of friends had parted ways. The Musica had gone westward to Mirt. There they snatched up cross-eyed twin brothers of fifteen years, both destined for the stocks or worse. In Ut, Ingo, by shadow, freed a midwife strung up in a tree while drunken villagers brawled between themselves. Lira rescued a windworker and a trunk of books from Leben fires, while daring Yda curled the blinding smoke into Lebenite eyes.

Ingamald recalled her own disappointing audience with Prince Ranðulfr in Ruheplatz.

"I cannot help you, Ingamald." Ranðulfr's eyes were hard.

"Prince, you are a friend to the people. And my friend. You never before harboured grudge or disdain for the meek, the crippled, the poor. You were never before afraid of magic. Jygaard is a sorceror in your employ."

"Jygaard grows old."

"Still, he is a mage. He practises magic. It is forbidden."

"Yes. But I am granted certain liberties."

"Listen to your own words. You are granted. You. A prince. What obeisance owe you to any man?"

Ran∂ulfr grew defensive. "There are many of Winter's edicts with which I agree, Ingamald. He is no fool."

"With what? With what do you agree, Ran∂ulfr?"

"Taxes. It costs much to run a kingdom, Ingamald. A certain degree of control needs be executed. The people do not know what always is best."

"Costs! Control! Executed! How can you use such ugly words? You a good and just man. Or at least you were..." Her eyes sparked.

"Mind your tone, Ingamald. You are my guest and in my protection."

"What say you, Prince?" Ingamald's head snapped and she drew herself up. "Protection? From what? Or whom? You, Ran∂ulfr?"

Ran∂ulfr shook his head. Regret tinged his voice. "I forget me. Ingamald, I am sorry. You have nothing to fear from me or mine."

"It is my hope, Prince." Moments passed. Ingamald looked at the young man slumped at his great table. "Fear you books and knowledge, too, Ran∂ulfr?"

"No." He shot her a look of unhappiness.

"Then what hold has Winter upon you?"

"He threatened," Ran∂ulfr swallowed. "He threatened first to harm my aging father. And then my sister, Gretchen. He promised to abduct her or worse, slit her throat in the night, should I not comply."

Ingamald remembered kindly King Rote and his daughter. She recalled Gretchen's gentle tone and manner, the siblings' devotion to each other. Ingamald revisited the day she awakened Prince Ranðulfr from a sleeping death with a witch's kiss.

"And you know, as do I, Ingamald, that Winter does what he will. His ways, his workers are duplicitous, insidious. He has so many in his service."

"Aye. I see." Ingamald's face grew softly sad. "You could have asked Jygaard for help. You could have asked me."

"I did ask Jygaard. He is old. He grows feeble-minded and fearful. And you... I could not fathom."

"Aye, Prince. You still do not fathom me, I fear."

"No. It is true. But I can offer you a haven. Here in Ruheplatz. In my castle."

"Locked in your tower with my hair to let down and bid you entrance?"

"No, Ingamald. Safely stowed from Winter's harm. He will find you and harm you, Ingamald. Be assured."

"I am assured. You asked me before, Prince. The answer is still the same. I am not for your keeping, nor any man's, I."

"Ah, Ingamald. Aye me."

Now again in the depth of winter in the heart of Bruë Wood, she frowned at recollection of this unfortunate conversation. Ranðulfr was irresolute and afraid. He was as good as Winter's puppet. None of this boded well.

Sighing, she returned her thoughts to Yule. The Troubadour and Erabesque had by now rejoined the Musica camp near Eiden; there the rescued would find temporary refuge. On their journey thence, the Troubadour delivered Hana to Nookeshea last Friday, and he had promised to return shortly. A beribboned charm under the tree awaited the Musica man. The witch hoped he would claim it on the morrow.

Soon, perhaps as soon as this storm passed, they would all be on their meandering ways once more. Ingamald glanced towards Hana, snoring softly. Anxiety clawed at her chest. If only she could keep the old woman closely by. But Hana would not hear of it, insisting that

Hören Village needed her protection. Independent and stubborn, the ancient wicca woman would return to her home with the aid of the Troubadour. Only last eve, she had waved away Ingamald's warnings.

"If I die, I die. I am not an immortal, Ingamald."

"Why need you die before your time?"

"Who are you to know my time? Aye, perhaps it does grow nigh. I am no kitten, you well know." Ingamald's shoulders sagged. Hana spoke again tenderly, "Pupil and daughter, weep not. Still I breathe. Still I am here. To help you. To love you. As I will beyond death. And mayhaps," she finished softly, "my small leave-taking will avert some grander peril."

So there was no arguing. Hana would journey home with the Troubadour. Ingamald, Yda and Lira, bound for Mountain Vale, would accompany them part way. Wily Ingo was already at large, sneaking about. The Troubadour and Erabesque would turn back to their tricks. The witch, the Learned woman, and the girl with fingers six and six, would carry on covertly from under Sall's roof. It would be good to see Sall at least, receive her hospitality, hear her news.

Ingamald tied the last stitch of the tapestry and cut the thread with her teeth.

"Since end of Yule, the latest clandestine ruses include," Didion cleared his throat, "one village idiot turned loose (village of Eiden), ten women prisoners suspected of malfeasance released (town of Doorne), seizure and confiscation of one cartload of books destined for the pyre (hamlet of Ekvil)." Sighing, the hunchback closed the ledger book from which he read. "No person knows where the intrepid malefactors next will strike."

Absorbed, Morton Winter stroked the ermine fur of his warming cloak. His eyes narrowed. He sniffed the chill chamber air. "Let us therefore up the ante threefold," he began mildly. "Let us make a prize for the capture of these vile culprits. Say, one hundred silver pieces on each miscreant head; one thousand for each witch."

Didion reopened the book and scribbled the command.

"Let us rob in secret as the fiends do. Let us go forth to the unsuspecting Hana of Hören Wood and snatch her in the night."

Didion's quill paused, midstroke. "A witch is not easily stolen in the night like some unattended treasure, Lord Winter." The hunchback glanced nervously at the fool, expressionless at the master's feet. "Where be a witch, magic be afoot."

"Then let us lie in wait until she drops her guard, Didion. She is old and addled. She will stumble and we will catch her." Morton still frequently consulted Tabula for glimpses of knowledge about Hana. Now even greater numbers of Winter's spies would be planted throughout Hören Wood. It was only a matter of time, he was certain.

"As you say."

"And finally, let it be known that in our own jaols are the greatest numbers in all of Hinterlünd. Boast that our dungeons are glutted with the creatures we despise: freaks and imbeciles, mischief and magic-makers, Rowan scum, itinerant cheats and swindlers. Announce these very same will be on display during the week of Carnival. That the law-abiding curious are invited to attend their trials," Morton Winter pursed his lips, "and their most public executions."

"As you say, my lord."

Morton drained the last of his glass, and selected another tasty from a small table beside him.

His fool raised an eyebrow. "Methinks not only your dungeons are gluttons."

Morton Winter chuckled cooly and reached again.

CHAPTER

A HEAVY IRON HOOK dangled precariously above their heads. It began to sway, though the wind was quiet. Nearby, Zem Jr., Piet and Gunter sat making tracks in the snow with their wooden blocks. But directly underneath, Sall's girls, Merelda the eldest and Freya, her younger sister, stood with hands on hips and tongues chattering, their voices shrill in chorus.

"Freak! Queer thing! How does yer mither stand the look o' ye?"

"The 'she' does not. Mother is dead." Yda spat.

"Sure, she died at yer birth at first look of ye!"

"Nay, the 'she' died of the plague I wish will visit you!" Yda concentrated more solidly on the grappling hook and its pulley. Just enough force would bring it crashing down upon the silly pates of these ugly 'shes'. Then the 'shes' would see and know that none should speak so to a girl with twelve fingers instead of ten.

"AVERT!" Ingamald's voice, loud and sudden, interrupted Yda's thought and deed.

The hook above their heads swung down dangerously, but halted just before its swaying arc could knock the girls senseless. A glance told the witch that the pulley and the lock which held the rope had been bent and damaged. She pushed the shrieking twosome out of harm's way and secured the rope to the barn door handle as Sall came running from the house.

Amid protests and tears tumbled the story.

"And where did ye learn such careless, cruel words, Freya? Fer shame it is. And Merelda, ye at better than ten years! Who taught ye to make jest of any folk? Yda is yer guest and mine." Sall shook her daughters. "Get some sense back into those wee heads of yourn."

Ingamald's eyes were feline in fury. "Yda! You could have killed Merelda and Freya. What would you then? We have spoken about using your power for good or ill."

"Those 'shes' spoke hate! Those 'shes' insulted Mother! And Yda, too!"

"It matters not what any say. What matters is what you do!"

Sall spoke up. "Yda, sorry am I for their misbehaviour."

Yda spluttered through her tears, "It little matters. I have heard tell all this before."

"That does not make it right. Nay, nor easier to bear. Ye may have an extra finger upon each hand, but these have an even greater affliction. Ill manners." Sall turned to her girls. "What say ye, both of ye?"

"We are sorry," sniffed Merelda.

"Aye, sorry." Freya's eyes were upon her feet.

Ingamald nudged Yda. Perplexed, the girl nudged back. Ingamald bent to her ear. "Apologies offered in sincerety should be so received."

Yda hissed back at her. "I do not believe for a moment these 'shes.'"

Sall took each daughter by the hand. "Well, I have a fine pile of washing suddenly needin' yer attention, girls." Not daring to whine, and newly nervous around Yda, they went willingly.

Ingamald turned to her young charge. "Yda was uncharitable. And her actions were worse. Is this the kind of girl you choose to become?"

"What? And should I be like you then? Always right. Always goody? Is that what you would wish? That I be goody like Ingamald is always?"

Annoyed, the young witch sharpened her tongue, "Forget you, then, Yda, that I ate my very mother? And I could, if I willed, eat you!"

Yda shot the witch a look locked between hate and terror. She leapt to her feet and darted away.

"Yda! I meant not..." Ingamald recalled her own tormented childhood, the malicious taunts of the village bratlings. Their parents' threat on her life. Her banishment. And her intense loneliness. The witch chastised herself and hurried after Yda.

She found her sitting miserable in the fork of an aged apple tree. Ingamald sat on her cloak on the snow, her face turned to the winter sun. "You see, Yda. Ingamald is not always good. And betimes not very wise."

"Words spoken can be cudgels."

"Well said, child. I am sorry for my words. I lost my better mind."

Yda was sullen and silent.

Ingamald mused aloud. "I could have gone her way. Spinne's. My mother's. The way of destruction and black arts. But I had Hana as guide. As real mother, even though she was not. And Hana taught me well. So well, that when Spinne offered to share with me her malevolence, her control and dominion over all, there was but one choice. I had to destroy her to save myself from becoming her.

"So you see that I worry for you likewise. I know you are not my daughter, still I recognize something of Ingamald in you. You have a gift. However you use or misuse the gift, in the end, will be up to you. I cannot write the book of Yda. You yourself hold the quill. But it is my dearest hope that therein you will write wisely. And I can teach you to write, Yda."

"I already know how to write. The Bookewoman taught me."

"Aye. But you are no simple. Yda knows what Ingamald means."

The child rubbed her hands over the bark of the slumbering apple tree. "Yda has ruined Zem's pulley."

"Yda can bend it aright again."

"Ingamald, do you really eat children such as Yda?"

"Nay, Yda. Only very young babes. They are much more tender."

"Ingamald!"

"I jest, child, I jest." Ingamald's laugh rang with mischief. This, she thought, is just how such rumours about the Craft begin.

Later, Ingamald examined carefully the hook and pulley, satisfied that Yda had mended well. Out of the corner of her witch's eye, she saw Merelda, with Freya in tow, approach Yda and offer her a bisquit. Yda accepted and soon all three girls were busy at play. Ingamald stood marvelling at the ways of children as Sall came up beside her.

"Sure, it's a mystery. As though no slight e'en happened."

"What be the secret children know and adults do not, Sall?"

"Aye, I wish they'd tell us all." Sall's smile melted to a frown. She bit her lip. "I think I have been a prattling fool, Ingamald."

Puzzled, the witch faced her friend.

"A dwarf came to call. Feeble with ague. We took him in. Well, I did. E'en though Zem objected. Nursed him back to health. A kind fellow, 'e is, this Dagnott. Lost. Hurt. A sadness about his eyes. But here's the thing," Sall swallowed, "I think my tongue wagged secrets I should not be tellin'."

"Howso, Sall?"

"Yer name, Ingamald," Sall half-sobbed. "I gave the dwarf yer name, lass! Aye, Sall did. Simpleton Sall."

"Nay, nay, Sall. Many know my name. Indeed, everyone in Wellhørst. Where's the harm?" Silently, she considered. Chances were that Morton Winter now knew her name. And perhaps more. "Whither did he go, this Dagnott?"

"He returned to his home, I should think. His people."

"To Voltan, then? Homeland of the dwarvish?"

"Nay...methinks he lives in Sprïggen, Ingamald. And I am afeared. Mayhaps he is a spy for the tyrant fiend of whom ye spoke last eve."

"You were right to tell me, Sall. Better to know than not. You did nothing wrong, dear friend." She embraced Sall then led her back to the house to share this news with Lira.

He was an old farmer with a leathern face cracked with crinkles. In each hand, a bucket of slops. He stood still, squinting at the three, woman and woman and child, before him.

"Cum it me, then. Hoory! Or 'ats after ye will be upon us all." He dropped the buckets and their contents sloshed over the ground.

Ingamald and Lira took ahold of one hand each of Yda and pulled her after the quickly retreating man.

"In 'ere!" He indicated the open door to the pigshed.

"Ooh, it stinks!" Yda shrank back.

"Hush, Yda!" Lira was frantic.

"It'll do for the loiks o' three felons like ye! Git!"

"I will not!" Yda stamped a stubborn foot.

Ingamald spun the girl into her gaze. "Aye, Yda, you will!" With a shove she thrust the girl inside and followed after.

The farmer bolted the door. "Now shut yer holes! I hear hooves approachin'!"

She put her witch's eye to a chink in the pigshed wall and watched as ten mounted horsemen galloped into the pig farmer's yard. They barked sharp requests at the humble man who shook his head and shrugged, then pointed elsewhere, eastward. In relief she watched the riders bound away; in regret she noted that they wore Prince Ranðulfr's colours.

"Ye need to stay in hidin' 'til the moon's up!" the farmer whispered hoarsely through the door. "You can stay in 'ere. What they want with three womenfolk I can only guess. Just don't put a wee spell on me pigs."

He trumped away, and the three fugitives sank into bales of straw. Their cramped quarters smelled horribly. Ingamald summoned up a small witchlight with a quick incantation. By its dim light, they spied a sow suckling her many babies in the corner of the shed. The she-pig grunted amiably.

"Ooh, look at the darlings!" Yda picked up a piglet.

Exhausted, Lira dropped to sleep. Ingamald fought off her fatigue, tried to stay alert. They had been running for days. From Sall's house to Hören Wood to somewhere east.

She knew Roc had followed them silently to Mountain Vale. Still she was startled when he brought the informant at knifepoint to the door of Sall's shed where the witch and her companions slept. The man, Todt, was persuaded by the tip of Roc's dagger to tell about the price on their heads, most especially her own and Hana's. He was only one of many who traversed the woods and all of Hinterlünd ready to seize opportunity and thus the silver reward. Todt, terrified witless, they set free. Ingamald lost no time in rousing the others. She left Sall wringing her hands, convinced of her responsibility for their jeopardy.

Next the small band made their way towards Hana's hut. A three-day journey became four with a child in tow. The witch's stomach twisted in apprehension. She wished for horses many times along the way. Lira and Yda wondered at Ingamald's newest, taciturn friend; they knew little about Rowan ways. However, Roc proved an indispensible scout and hunter and uncertainty quickly turned to admiration.

As they drew nearer Hören Wood and Hana's cottage, Ingamald's alarm cooled to a calm dread. She knew that her mentor was gone. Taken. As they reached the humble dwelling, its door askew, she kept the others back, entered alone. Inside there was no suggestion of any struggle. All the dishes were clean and neatly put away. Hana's bed was made and undisturbed. The tapestry woven by

Ingamald's witch fingers hung slightly crooked on the wall. Hana had gone willingly. Ingamald sensed it. How else could they have taken her? A spell of concealment was woven round this cottage. For some reason, Hana had stepped beyond its protection. What had the old woman foreseen to have chosen such an act of willful surrender? Ingamald staunched her tears, beckoned the others inside.

"We will rest us here and decide what to do on the morrow." Lira lit a fire in the desolate hearth and Ingamald wandered into the trees, Roc beside her. She happened upon a bush of nettles. Caught therein the royal hues of purple and gold, a piece of fabric torn from some soldierly costume.

"The Prince's men, Roc. Prince Ranðulfr has stolen Hana."

The Rowan man said nothing.

In the night, he came to her with bloodied hands.

"Roc!" Ingamald pulled him into the cottage, slamming the door. "What have you done?"

"Killed."

"Whom, Roc? Whom have you killed?"

"One who sought to kill Ingamald. Now you must go. The woods are full of men."

The three dressed hurriedly, packed a little food, vaulted into the darkness.

"You must come with us, Roc."

"I will be decoy."

"Roc, I forbid this foolishness!" Wordless, the Rowan man backed away from Ingamald and slipped invisible into the dark trees. The witch wove a cover of shadow to camouflage the threesome. In this way, they slipped soundlessly through Hören Wood, past villagers with torches, men with silver aglint in their nocturnal eyes. For a second time in her life, Ingamald ran from her childhood home.

Since those few sleeping hours in Hana's abandoned hut, they had slept but middling. Stolen winks here and there in the day under cover of cave or thicket. Scant food supplemented by handfuls of berries, gobbled hurriedly. Hunted, they ran. Ingamald knew not why but took the direction of Ruheplatz. Somehow she must reason with Ranðulfr. Win Hana's freedom even to sacrifice her own. And somehow she would make Lira and Yda safe. She little knew how.

Panic had pursued them for days. Panic and men. Bedraggled and famished, the three footsore escapees pressed desperately onwards. Ingamald's thoughts were a maze. Her empty stomach churned anxiously. Her heart lurched at Yda's weeping, but the young witch seemed at a loss for any spell or word of calm. The spectre dread haunted her, waking or sleeping.

Here in a pigshed came at last clarity. Jumbled tossing fears abated somewhat. Her heartbeat slackened. Ingamald sat still enough to reshape her thoughts and plan afresh.

Outside the Prince's men. Inside the child now asleep, cuddling a sleeping piglet. Lira lost in dream. A few quick steps away, the helpful pig farmer and mayhaps hope.

Ingamald worked a charm and the bolt slipped from its place. She stepped out, rebolted the door, and darted over to the homely farmhouse. The farmer sat warming his arthritic hands around a cup of tea as Ingamald entered his dwelling.

"What? Woman, are ye daft? What did I tell ye?"

"What are you called, farmer?"

"Wilm."

"I am Ingamald, Farmer Wilm. I thank you for your saving of us." She recalled that morn as the three dashed across an open field, tripping through the snow, desperately seeking shelter from the riders who'd caught sight of them in the trees. This man had not been afraid of two women and a child. "Now I ask what you might most need?"

Wilm scratched his greying head, then looked at the liver spots on his hands. "Guess I'd wish away this cursed swellin' were't I could."

Ingamald went to the window, surveyed the farmyard in the winter afternoon light. She pointed out the dried berries on bushes along his fence. “There, Wilm, see you. Grind those berries to powder. Add to your tea and drink. The pain and swelling will abate.”

“Ye’re a witch or somat then?”

“Aye.”

“As was me grandymither. Glad I am that she is dead and gone afore this weary awful toime. Come to think on’t. She used those berries for any number o’ ailments. It’s a thick head does not remember a wise woman’s wisdom.”

“Any craft takes practice. I suspect my ways with pigs would be severely wanting.”

Wilm chuckled in agreement.

“I have one other favour to ask. I must leave my friends now, Wilm. Could you... could you see to it that they are safely stowed here on your farm? Could you...mayhaps put on that they are your daughter and granddaughter?”

“Sposen I do. Sposen those damnable riders cumit back. Does this look loik a house wiv womenfolk in’t?”

Ingamald studied the barren walls, the mismatched crockery, the lumpish bed. “Nay, it does not. But I have faith in Lira and young Yda that they could give it their best women’s touch.”

“’Ow long they be stayin’ then?”

“A fortnight or longer, Wilm.”

He paused to light his pipe. “Well, witch. ’Ere’s the thing then. Bring some o’ that foin tobaccy from the city wi’ ye next toime yer in ’ese parts, an’ ye’ve a deal.”

“Aye! Done!” Ingamald’s eyes were emerald and certain. With a tilt of her chin and a quick wave, she left Wilm preparing for winter berry-picking.

Within the hour they found her. Wandering in the open field. Ten men rode up and encircled her, threw a rope net over her, trussed her up and tossed her into the tumbrel. Twelve frigid days they rode rough over the winter paths towards Ruheplatz. At night, they tied her tautly to the cartwheel just close enough to the fire to keep her from freezing. Threw her scraps as though she were any mongrel dog.

Daytime, the fettered witch jounced along the rough boards of the cart so that every inch of her was either bruised or scraped. Her captors refused to stop even briefly, and so she sat in garments soaked and soiled.

Forced to endure such humiliation, Ingamald felt her witch's blood roil. But each time her spine tingled with temper, or her fingers itched to work a spell against the ruffians, she fought against the urge, even biting her tongue against any charm of unbinding.

"Surrender," she whispered hoarsely to herself. "Hana saw some profit in it. So must you be likewise patient and steadfast." And so she withstood the cold, her terror and her maltreatment.

At the end of twelve days Ingamald lay stupified, half-delirious, filthy, and bleeding from her ropes. The posse trotted triumphantly into Ruheplatz. Citizens greeted them to jeer at her. At last, they paraded into the castle courtyard of frail King Rote and the son who ruled for him.

"Zounds, men! This is no way to treat her! Release her at once!" The voice was familiar, and Ingamald allowed herself a speck of hope.

Later, she awoke in a great bed, Gërt's anxious face hovering overhead. The maidservant fed her broth, bathed her limbs, applied salve to her chafed wrists and face. Weakly, Ingamald dressed in the proffered clean clothes, and heedless of Gërt's protests, sought out the royal antechamber. Prince Ranðulfr sat on his throne, Karenina, his wife, at his side. He was bent in consultation with one of his ministers and looked up in surprise at her arrival.

"Ingamald."

"I would speak with you, Prince."

"Do you think it wise, Ingamald? You are weak and have been ill-used. I have reprimanded the men. Take a day. Or two. Let us parley then."

"Now, Ranðulfr."

The prince looked uncomfortable. He dismissed his minister who bowed away. "My dear?" He smiled at Karenina who nodded demurely to him and to Ingamald and left them alone.

"Where is Hana?" Ingamald's tone made Ranðulfr wince.

"Ingamald, be reasonable."

"Tell me, Prince. Or I swear I will spoil that child growing in Karenina's womb."

Ranðulfr blanched. "Hana is gone. Taken. To Sprïggen."

"You surrendered her."

"Yes." The Prince's reply barely audible.

Ingamald stood smouldering before Ranðulfr. She swallowed the spell of impotency she yearned to cast on him. "Wherefore? Whyso?"

"I am wretched and weak, Ingamald. Morton Winter has taken Gretchen. Just as he promised. It was a bargain, Ingamald. Gretchen for Hana."

The witch snorted. "And have you Gretchen back with you again?"

"No. No. She is not returned to us. Her husband, Lord Field has gone to plea for her release." Ranðuflr hung his head.

"You promised ne'er to hurt me or mine."

"Yes."

"You have violated that trust."

"I know it."

"Give me then the means to leave Ruheplatz. A sturdy horse at midnight beyond the city walls."

"I cannot. You are under house arrest, Ingamald." Forthwith, the prince clutched at his throat, choking. He began to turn red.

"Merely grant me my suit and live." Ingamald's voice and face were expressionless.

Helplessly, Ranðulfr clutched the air. Desperate, he nodded, and instantly the spell was lifted. He gasped for breath. "In peril you leave, Ingamald."

"Foolish Prince. Everything I do is perilous. She turned on her heel to the left. "Do not fail me, Prince Ranðulfr. Remember the child in your wife's womb. If the babe matters not enough, remember your own cowardly neck. Fail me not at midnight."

Gërt snaked through the darkened streets of Ruheplatz city with Ingamald close behind. The women kept to the shadows. As midnight bells tolled, they reached the city gates.

"Good luck be with you, Ingamald."

"And you, Gërt, ever my friend and caregiver."

Gërt stepped from the shadows towards the surly doorkeeper.

"Who goes there?"

"Only Gërt, man. Come to see you."

Grunting, the brawny man came forward, grabbed the maidservant in his thick arms and began feverishly kissing her neck. Wrapped in her green mantle, Ingamald slinked past them, unlocked the small gatekeeper's door and closed it again. Outside a fine mare stood saddled and waiting.

Ingamald mounted. The black mare neighed once. The witch spoke soft into the horse's left ear. Then, cape flying, hair askew and aflame in the moonlight, witch and horse sped away posthaste from the betrayal of Ruheplatz.

CHAPTER

INGAMALD SMELLED THE SMOKE before she saw the ruined shell that was Nookeshea.

She urged the black mare into a canter along the forest floor. They broke through the trees to the clearing. At its heart a fumid wreck.

Gone was her strong oaken door. The entranceway gaped black. Her roof was entirely destroyed, its thatch having quickly succumbed to the first flames. Part of the north wall had caved in. Nookesheas's windows were sad burnt out eyes. Ingamald approached her devastated home, despair thick in her throat.

The spell of security about her abode had faltered in her too-long absence.

Within the broken stone circle, the snow was filthy with charred detritus, some of it still smouldering. The root cellar doors were torn from their hinges and the contents had been plundered. Ingamald dismounted and willed her feet towards what had been her home. She entered wounded Nookeshea.

Retching at the sickening smoke that still swirled within, the witch rummaged through the remains. Shards of shattered pottery littered the floor. Remnants of blackened furniture, dismembered, lay strewn about. Every piece of clothing turned to ashes. All her meagre possessions torched.

Who would set Nookeshea aflame? None but Winter's vassals. Who would have told them where to find and destroy her haven? Only the folk of Wellhørst. Another betrayal. Whom could a witch trust?

As if in answer to her unspoken question, Roc stepped noiselessly into the skeleton of her cottage. Simultaneously, Beezle, bedraggled and besooted, dragged himself from beneath a pile of rubble, meowing and miraculously unhurt. In the usual if fusty corner, she spied stalwart Broom Hildë, defiant survivor of the violators.

Ingamald scooped up her cat and wept into his black fur. She walked with broom and familiar into the weak morning light.

"Many men came, brandishing torches, and I could do nothing."

"Aye, Roc," she managed. "It is not your fault."

"Both our homes destroyed by fire." The Rowan man kicked snow onto a bit of flaming winterweed. It hissed and died.

There was naught to do but attend to the other small flames and glowing embers scattered about the circle. Ingamald released Beezle who immediately found a winter sun ray and began to groom. The black mare neighed plaintively.

"She is thirsty and needs unsaddling." Ingamald's voice cracked.

"A fine beast."

"Aye."

"I will tend to her."

Ingamald ensured that the stone circle was remade intact. Walking widdershins, she cast a spell of quandary. If others came a-riding by with violent or murderous intent, they would grow confused near this place, double back and lose themselves. She gathered kindling and started a fire anew in the centre. To this she added pieces and bits, burning up the remaining debris of her life.

She and Beezle sat warming themselves when Roc returned, leading the mare. He threw her saddle safely aside, tethered her to a tree and offered her wild oats.

"What is she called?" He stroked the mare's neck.

"Night." Ingamald shivered. "But this is no day to be out of doors for horse or man or cat or witch."

"Pine boughs."

"What mean you?"

"Over the cellar. Over the cottage. Shelter from the wind and winter. Shelter for witch and cat. And Night, the mare."

Ingamald nodded. "Good. Let us work then. I have no patience for indolence."

Each with a knife in hand, witch and Rowan man spent much of the day hewing pine boughs, fashioning makeshift roofs for Nookeshea and the root cellar. The cottage was malodorous, but the horse seemed not to mind. The underground cellar proved less so, and while cramped, was dry and apt. By nightfall, all was made ready. Ingamald and Roc munched on dried meat, sharing morsels with ravenous Beezle. The fire in the stone circle offered a friendly blaze in contrast to what had transpired two nights hence.

The weary wicca woman yawned twice. Roc rose to leave.

"Where go you, Roc?"

"To my dwelling, deep in this forest."

Ingamald raised her face to the moon. "The world has come undone, Roc. I can make no sense of it tonight." She turned her green eyes on him. "I would you would stay here. As would Beezle and Night." She touched his braid.

In the morning she rose before him.

Her cat glided out after her into the daylight. "Beezle, I must away again. Stay with Roc. Stay here. When I return, you and I will make repairs and begin afresh."

Ingamald took Broom Hildë in hand. With her travelling pouches over her left shoulder, she mounted the sturdy elderwood handle. "Fly Hildë!"

The broom shuddered and sighed upwards. Ingamald circled once round the clearing. Roc crawled out from the root cellar in time to see the witch careen westward away. In his hand, he held a lock of her copper hair.

She landed three leagues from Sprïggen, determined to go the rest of the way afoot, so safely stowed Broom Hildë in the upper branches of a spruce. Ingamald spun resolutely on her heel to the left.

"Winter, I come! Whether you will it or no. As with you, so with me: fire and ice with ice and fire!"

CHAPTER

MORTON WINTER BURPED LOUDLY his satisfaction. Before him were scattered the carcasses of two roasted fowl. He dipped his ringed fingers in the finger bowl a servant held, dried them on the towel over the arm of another.

Hana of Hören Wood was stowed securely, deep in a Sprïggen Castle dungeon. She had not spoken. Yet. But perhaps tomorrow. After another night with the rats and other nightcrawlers.

Winter reached a plump white hand for a piece of fruit. Delicious.

The pale lord adjusted his expansive girth. Admired the many rings on his fat fingers. One for each of the executed thus far. His alchemist proved genius at turning carbon and ash and bone into these fine gemstones. Then Dagnott fastened them in the clever settings Winter himself designed. Each ring was a memento apropos of time well spent.

He pondered which instrument of torture would best suit Hana of Hören Wood. The scold's bridle? Pincers? Certainly the witch's chair. Most definitely accompanied by the device. A thrill fluttered through his body. She would be the first to behold it. In truth, it was an honour befitting her, if she were truly the powerful witch of rumour and gossip.

Craft of the Wise! Abhorrence soured his mouth. He spat copiously into the silver spittoon. Well, the other witch, the one called Ingamald, was sure to follow. Now that her house was roasted to a crisp. Morton Winter suspected that somehow the two wicca women knew each other, but the accursed hag would say neither aye or nay.

Tomorrow she would speak. His delicious device would loosen her tongue.

Yes, he would have a very special ring made up from the ashes of Hana of Hören Wood. An adroit design. And he would wear it always. Winter summoned the nearest servant to fetch him drawing paper, quill and ink.

Hana lay in the dark and listened. Dungeons have many sounds. During the day, shriek of metal on metal from the nearby smithy. Somewhere else, the chamber, she supposed, human cries of pain and terror. The slamming of iron-barred doors. At night, the sounds were different, no less pitiful. Screams from nightmare and nightfear. Moans of suffering, torment. Chains rattling. Scuttle of rodent and many legged creatures across her cell.

Sometimes the prisoners talked to each other. Hana had tried this also her first nights. No response from the cell to the left. But a woman on the right had spoken. A midwife suspected of witchery sobbed out her innocence. Hana did her best to calm her with words. With spells. But her spells could not hold when she was so weak. She hadn't seen much beyond water this day. Yesterday, a crust of bread.

She moved her body gingerly. It ached from the dampness of the place and her mistreatment. To be so old and so used. If she could only summon her strength tomorrow, she might manage an incantation to thwart the fiend Winter. But it was so difficult to centre her thoughts, her waning energy. And her memory, when she needed it most, was failing her.

Had she known the man in motley this afternoon? The fool present at her audience with Morton Winter? Or was an old and abused mind playing tricks? The hunchback, the dwarf, the others were strangers. But the jester. So familiar. It was important to remember. His bells and jests jangled her nerves. A memory inchoate flickered at the edge of her consciousness. She drifted.

Bells jangling anew woke her. Not bells but keys. Torchlit, someone walked towards her cell with a ring of keys. She heard the scraping of skeleton key in rusted lock. It resisted, then turned with a clang; hinges screeched at the opening. Hana shrank back into the shadows.

"Give me leave an hour, Didion." A misshapen figure nodded in the half-light, closed the protesting cell door and departed.

The figure in her dungeon chamber set his torch in the wall then turned to face the witch cowering. "Fear me not, Hana of Hören Wood. And friend."

From beneath his great velvet robe he produced a woolen blanket, bread, cheese and ale. With filthy hands she took these from him silently, nodding her thanks.

It was difficult to eat with swollen mouth and broken teeth. Still Hana devoured the offerings. She wiped her grimy face clear of crumbs and wrapped the woolen about her slight, chilled frame, hoping the cover would deflect her stench of seven days dungeon-spent.

"I would offer you hazeldean tea, but you see that my cupboards here are very bare," Hana told her visitor, espying him with her unblackened left eye.

"Aye, Hana. I would remove you from this place," he intoned despondently, "if I but could. I, too, am a prisoner."

"You are a fool, I think."

"Aye. On so many levels, old woman."

The pitch of his voice sent her reeling back years more than five and twenty. Through the cobwebs of her memory she remembered a younger man, vital. Good and prudent. Leader of the Congress of the

Light. A sorceror seduced by a sorceress. Trapped in her web, blind and poisoned. By Spinne. Ingamald's spider-mother.

"Welome to my cage, Svalbaard the Just, Master Wizard."

"Just Svalbaard now, Hana, and wizard never more."

"You were blind and babbling when we left you on the Isle of Arl. How came you here to this tyrant?"

"Like you, I am stolen. Or rescued. By Morton Winter. Arl is a windswept cold island, Hana."

"I know it."

"My keepers were little interested in my keeping. So I sought what healing I could without help or magic. I found herbs and I bubbled tinctures. To cure the venom of Spinne's sting. To settle my addled wits. My eyes grew clearer. And then I fashioned these lenses." He pushed his spectacles up the bridge of his nose. "My wits, however, remain less than clear." He chortled, then coughed wetly.

"In the end, my wit or witlessness, take whichever you choose, brought me to Winter, or to his attention. He journeyed as a younger man to Arl, seeking the colder climes which please him. And found me sputtering and muttering about the village Arling. He took me for a fool."

"Eh?"

"To be his fool. For fooling. Tomfoolery. I amuse him. And incense him. And placate and frustrate. Surely you know the jesterly tradition, Hana. Thus have I been in his employ ever since. If I disobey him, he will send me back to lonely Arl…or worse. I ran once and felt the cat o' nine tails on my back. I have not tried again since. So I found another way to subversion. After a time, perhaps seven years or more, I became the alchemist."

"Alchemist and fool, then?"

"Aye, an interesting counter-disguise, is it not? Spinne drained my life-magic; I can no longer be wizard. But I can read, and I did and do. Alchemy is my new craft, a fascinating study of life's properties.

"Morton Winter does not know fool and chemist are one man. He thinks the alchemist a half-mad recluse. He's not far off, I suppose. Heard whispered rumours of my secrets and mixtures. Saw my shadow in that cursed black table he consults to keep tabs on all of us.

"One day he summoned the alchemist. Sent emissaries to my small dwelling on the hill beyond the castle keep. I refused to see him, although I shook in my boots at his summons, I tell you. But I sent him a scroll declaring that I would work to solve any of the great natural mysteries for him and in his name, if only he would leave me to work in peace and anonymity."

"Winter agreed?"

"He wrote up a contract which I signed with my own blood. But yes. In his own cool fashion, he agreed to let me labour alone. He provides me with confiscated books. Indeed, I've amassed quite a library. And Winter seems to have accepted the mystery of the alchemist as he accepts the mystery of the Tabula."

"Tabula?"

"The great stone in his keeping of which I spoke. His object of lust and desire. An obsidian table that details what was and what is. How he came by it… by her, I know not. She is his great spying tool—mayhaps the very means by which he first spied you, Hana—but her mastery eludes him."

"I have heard tell of such speaking stones."

"Such magic he allows because it is for his gain. Winter sees alchemy likewise as profitable magic. Which I suppose it is, of a kind."

"What if someday the pale villain breaks the contract? Insists on an audience with his slaving alchemist?"

Svalbaard shrugged. "If he does so, I swore to steal away elsewhere and always. To take my great knowledge with me."

"Thus ever after playing the fool."

"Aye. Forever trapped in motley, I would have to abandon my study to save my foolish neck. However, one thing works to my alchemic advantage. While Winter despises and loathes learning, still he wishes to possess it all and, therefore, does not wish to lose his alchemist. So his whiteness accepts my reclusive wishes."

"A deviant who burns books desires knowledge?" Hana's damaged face was further flummoxed.

"I offer more than knowledge. I offer what he most wants to know. I promise him an elixir."

"As in the legends."

"Aye, it is that which he most seeks. The elixir of immortality. I pretend to work away at this complex and difficult task. Another ruse. In truth, I seek a means to destroy him. And as the tyrant has fatted on his conquests, I wax in wisdom to work his end."

"Why then do you not?"

"I have tried. He has poison tasters. Spies. Informants."

"Those like I met in Hören Wood." Hana paused to drink from the bottle of ale. "You, his fool, are so close to the man. Can you not steal into his chamber? Lean over his throne? Slip up behind him? Slit his whitish throat?"

"I have thought this. Wished it. Dreamed it. I have not seen opportunity…" Svalbaard looked into his hands.

"Morton Winter is close guarded. He seldom leaves his chamber. Never unaccompanied. And when alone in his private room, he is tight-buttressed. No one gains admission after the last servant takes leave each evening—no one save trusted Didion the hunchback, and he only occasionally when bidden. Winter sees to it that the dwarf plays locksmith and changes the locks frequently. And I am no lockpick.

"I could secret myself in the folds of the arras and murder him in the night. I have considered this. Desired it. But…I cannot risk it. If I try and fail, Tabula may tell. And I would not live out the day. Thus I must be sure the means I use are certain. I turn to my books, my study, for some future answer." Svalbaard paused, unhappy.

"I fear the man, Hana. And in my fear, my imprisonment. I have witnessed…" The alchemist looked away from the witch.

"Aye. His torture. His methods."

"It is why I have come this eve. I cannot secret you away. I risk Tabula's telling even with this visit. But I could not let the night pass, knowing what it is you face on the morrow."

A yelp rang out from a nearby cell.

"I am not afraid of death. I am an old woman, Svalbaard. Let death come."

"Not his kind of death, Hana the wise. I bring you a potion. A poison sure and swift. Bitter but painless. Take it when you will. An hour and your heart is stilled. Better swallowed tonight than tomorrow. Forego the agony. Spare yourself that much."

She accepted the vial. "And if Tabula shows to Winter your complicity in my death, what will you then?"

"The alchemist will disappear. In his place, merely a fool."

"How is it that this she-stone has not unmasked your disguise?"

Svalbaard shrugged. "Fool's luck? I can only hope she will keep my secret. She seems never to show him all but a part of events past and present. Neither does Tabula tell the future. Morton Winter does not command the stone. She commands Morton Winter."

Hana pocketed the vial. "I thank you for this small mercy, Svalbaard."

The alchemist said nothing, but turned to go.

"Tell her I love her, when you see her, as I know you will, Svalbaard."

"Whom?"

"Your daughter, the witch Ingamald. She lives."

"I did not dare to ask. To hope."

"Spinne is destroyed. By your daughter."

"I heard the tales. Wh-when is she come?"

"Soon, if I read rightly the signs just before my capture."

Svalbaard's shoulders drooped beneath their velvet. He opened the cell door. "Thanks for this news, Hana. I wish you good speed to the next world. I am sorry to do so little."

"Remember me to your daughter, Svalbaard."

"I will." Didion approached to lock anew the wretched door. Svalbaard winced at the metallic outcry.

"He will surely kill her." The alchemist did not give voice to this desolate thought or the next. "Morton Winter will kill my only child. My daughter. Ingamald."

Glinting silver and precise against the white cloth, an array of hand-sized instruments. Clamp, pick, chisel, drill, hammer, pincers, screws, vice. Delicate they seemed in the light of the torches. Morton salivated over his next selection. He drank deeply from a shiny flask, replaced it inside his thick robe, reached for the pincers.

Rarely now did he venture to the inmost corridors of his castle. His behemoth size made the going arduous; his fleshy legs protested any ascent or descent. But this Hana of Hören Wood was a special case. Thrice had she been brought to him after treatment, without satisfactory result. This time, Winter knew he himself must play interrogator.

She knelt before him in her rags. A servant stood by with perfumed handkerchief in case the master swooned. Didion sat with open book and quill poised to record the confession. At the far end of the room, draped in silver gauze, glittered the device. Beside it the dwarf. All was ready.

"Well, Witch. We have wasted three episodes with you. We are tired of your reticence in matters concerning our state. You are accused of witchcraft, a crime you do not deny, nor are willing to relinquish. Such practice is expressly forbidden in Hinterlünd."

"By whose authority?" Hana croaked.

"Mine own, insolent one!"

"I do not recognize your authority. No one commands or controls Hinterlünd."

Those gathered in the room gasped audibly. Morton Winter sniffed once. Nodded to a large man in black mask. A crack of a whip sounded. Hana hunched over, but emitted no sound.

Morton Winter began heating the pincers over a brazier of hot coals. “Woman, you need only tell us the names of your accomplices, those marauders with whom you consort.”

Hana was silent.

At a pallid summons from Winter, Dagnott began wheeling the device nearer the wiccan woman’s prostrate form. The pincers in the brazier glowed.

“Only say the names of those you protect and you will be spared.” Morton stepped towards Hana. The black-masked man seized her hair, raising her roughly back to kneeling.

“Tell us what Ingamald is to you, stinking crone!” Winter’s breath misted menace. He brought the pincers near enough for Hana to feel their white heat, raised his other arm in preparation for signal to Dagnott.

The dwarf steadied himself against the device, grabbed the drape in readiness. He had been drinking ale much of the night and most of the morning, a newly-acquired habit. He felt certain to vomit.

“I command you to use your black arts to bring her hither, hag! Otherwise, feel my wrath!” The pincers were nearly touching Hana’s flesh. Already it blistered in anticipation.

Hana turned her one wise eye upon the villain. She looked into his beady pale gaze and saw panic behind his intent. She gave a gravel chuckle. “May you get what you want, Morton Winter.”

And Hana slipped from life.

Winter gulped in disbelief. Death was Hana’s final defiance; he despised her the more for it. Enraged, he cast her corpse to the floor. Pitched the pincers across the room, narrowly missing Didion.

“Throw the witch on the fire!”

As quickly as his fattened form could accommodate him, Morton Winter quitted the chamber, a flock of servile placaters close behind him.

Dagnott lurched from the room, bent on losing himself in the roar of the first day of Carnival. Just beyond the castle walls, a maddened throng danced about the waiting stake. He did not pause when he heard their cackling outburst accompanying the lighting of the fire. Instead the dwarf twisted resolutely through the swelling crowds to the alehouse. Once inside, he put his hands over his ears in a vain attempt to quiet the disgusting tempest within and without.

CHAPTER

CROWS FLEW GYRES AGAINST THE SLATE SKY above the castle. A single light shone through the lead pane of the tower reach. The witch considered the prospect, her emerald eyes glowering. With a swoosh of Broome Hildë she could be tapping at that window. In the quickly fading light she could hover near the sill and frighten Morton Winter to death when he threw open the sash. That or stab him in the heart with her dagger, then spin away on her broom, witch-cackling under the new night moon.

But this was the fancy of folktale. Broom Hildë was safely stowed and Ingamald no malevolent crone of lore. She stood amongst the jostling crowds of Sprïggen masqueraders, her own new-bought mask raised above her sweating brow.

"Pssst. You moight want to tuck up that 'air and pull down that masque, if you 'ope to keep that 'ead o' yours then."

"Ingo!" Ingamald thanked the fates for her good fortune and adjusted the whiskered half-mask over her emerald cat-eyes. The fire-eater blinked out at her through a crescent moon façade.

"Follow me, Puss-in-Boots!"

She watched his fluttering cape and bright yellow hose as he threaded through the phalanx of people. Then will o' the wisp, he disappeared. Frantically, she searched the masked faces. None was the colour, the shape of the man of the moon. Ingo was gone. Vanished. A snuffed flame.

Ingamald felt the certain crush of revellers. Foreign tongues rang out. Weird music rose above her head. She found it hard to breathe. Onwards she pushed, unmindful of her direction. First an errant turn here. Around a false corner there. She wrenched herself against the current of the crowd. Turned again. Again. And again until dizzy. The only thing now was to escape the foul-smelling air. The madly grinning masks. The screams and shrieks of the carnival pulsing to climax.

"Ingo?" The witch thrust through the thickness of festive rabblerousers. Someone wrenched her cape. Some oaf trod on her toe. Fingers picked at her cloak pocket. The clutch and claw of too many in the unsavory street roused nausea and panic.

"Ingo!" Her cry was swallowed in the hubbub. She tried to slow her heartbeat, steel her mind. Breathless, trapped, she could do nothing now but surrender to the will of the mob foisting her gleefully, crazily towards nowhere and everywhere. The edges of her vision distorted; the witch swam a whirling, blurry vortex.

A sudden shrill whistle sounded. Above the carousers' heads, dazzling lights burst eastwards in the sky.

Ingo. Through dim consciousness, Ingamald instinctively propelled her reeling self easterly. Crackling skywards, several shooting star fireworks beckoned her noisily.

"Ingo!"

"In 'ere, witch!" A grimy hand snatched her wrist and hauled her into a darkened portal. A quick key to a lock and a slamming of the door. Ingo's nimble fingers flashed a flame, and he led her up a stairwell to a second door. He opened this too, pushed her in, and locked the door securely. In a breathspan, he raced over to the open window and slammed it shut, drawing the drape to shut out the din and glare of the wild cavorters in the street below. With a finger's snap, he lit a single candle. Fire-eater and witch stood breathless, facing each other.

"If Winter foinds you, 'e will kill you or worse, Ingamald! An' 'is spies are everywhere!"

"He has taken Hana. He has torched Nookeshea. What further injury could he do me?"

"Nookeshea is burned?"

"Nigh to the ground, Ingo."

"Damn that white rat!"

"So you see there is little more to fear."

"Lookit, Ingamald, there's much more and you know it! Winter devises tortures. Burns wimmin—especially witchfolk loik you at the stake. Some poor wench burned yesterday. An 'e knows our very movements. Prob'ly already knows you're 'ere."

Ingamald drew a shaky breath to calm her mind. "No, Ingo. I think not yet."

"Well soon then, Ingamald. Morton Winter 'as a table, black as noight. Tabula. It tells 'im what 'e wants most to know. An' 'e wants most to know about you."

"Then it will serve me better to know him first. I will enter Sprïggen Castle a second time."

"Are you mad, too?"

"Aye. Mad and a witch."

Ingo clucked his tongue. "Not tonoight, Ingamald. You'll need vittles and sleep to keep your wits." The fire-eater pulled a loaf of dark coarse bread and a jug of water from a rough cabinet against the wall.

They sat to sup at the crude table.

"Be there a charnel house or house of pox within these city walls?"

Ingo choked on a dry crust. Recovering, he managed to sputter, "What're you thinkin', Ingamald? To rob the dead? Work a few cures and call more attention to yourself? Or merely die o' the plague?"

"Say aye or nay, Ingo, and if aye, say where."

"Aye, aye! I'll take you there under cover o' darkness though I'm befuddled by your logic, witch. While you're at it, why don't you just sell copies o' your grimoire on the street corner to earn a few pennies on the soid?"

"My books of spells are char and ash, else would I!" Ingamald drank deeply from the bottle and wiped the last of the crumbs from her homespun. "Have you heard tell of our other friends, Ingo?" The wicca woman picked at the lint on her skirt.

"The Musica are three or so hours beyond the western walls of the city."

"Have you seen the Troubadour? Talked with him?"

"Briefly. 'E don't much care for me, I'm afraid, me witch friend. Bit 'o rivallry, way I figures. Dunno why. It's obvious 'oo's the better man."

"Where are Lira and Yda, Ingo?"

"Safe and sound in one of 'em caravans, leastways that's wha' I saw wi' me one venture out there."

Ingamald sighed in relief. "When will the Musica enter the city?"

"They await your word."

"Tell them...tell them I am here and not to come into the city proper."

"If you think that gold-toothed rogue will listen to me tell 'im what to do..."

"Take this to him then." Ingamald pulled ink, quill and parchment from one of her leather pouches. Hastily, she scribbled a message and signed the paper boldly, sealing it with wax from the smoking candle.

"'E won't be 'appy."

"We none of us are happy, Ingo." The witch rose to shake out her green cloak and hang it on a wall peg. Her voice was thoughtful. "When is it safest to quit your room, Ingo?"

"You mean besoids never? Within the witching hour, witch. After most o' the revellers have tripped along home an' only the stragglers and us vagabond performers remain in the dirty streets."

"Aye. We vagabonds." Ingamald's back was still towards the fire-eater.

"Aye. I s'pose practitioners o' the craft qualify as vaga... Blimey!!" Ingo stood gape-mouthed at the mirror image turning to face him.

"Well, Ingo? What think you? Am I sufficiently of your likeness?"

Stunned, the fire-eater could only nod dumbly at his exact replica.

"I cannot manage to duplicate your tangle tongue. But if I keep my mouth shut and my thoughts to myself, no one will be the wiser, will they now?"

"'Ow did you? 'Oo taught you to shapeshift to become Ingo?"

"This is no shape-shifting, but illusion." Her witch's voice spoke through his twin's lips.

"Regardless, this gives me a bit o' th' creepies, if you don't moind me sayin', Ingamald. It's loik lookin' at me very self."

"Don't much like what you see?" Ingo-Ingamald smiled.

"Actually, I thought I was better lookin'. Truth to tell, I'm a little disappointed."

Ingamald pulled Ingo over to the looking glass. "Well, if we clean our teeth and cheeks, matters would be much improved."

"Thank you, witch. I'll look to that once you're out o' me 'air."

"We might want to run a comb through that, too."

"I'll make sure me personal groomer sees to that, as well."

Witch and fire-eater beheld each other and burst into a wry joint chuckle, interrupted by the toll of a midnight bell.

"Take me thither to the sick house, Ingo."

"Righto, Ingomald. Step this way."

Darting carefully into the street, twin Ingos worked their wary way to the Pox Inn, a last refuge for the sick and dying citizens of Sprïggen. Part hospice, part morgue, here were housed the desperate and the desperately ill, those castaways within the walls of Winter's burg.

The fire-eater turned a corner and was gone, leaving his double to reassemble in a witch's blink as her former self. She rapped the heavy doorknocker, a grinning skull, thrice upon the door.

Gruff voices sounded within. The door creaked open a crack. A single candle flame pushed close to Ingamald's face.

"Who goes there? Friend or foe?"

"Friend. A healer. I bring herbs."

"Come in, then. Quickly now. Don't let the rats or worse in with you."

The speaker was a hunched old woman, bowed by perhaps sixty or more years of hard living.

"How did you get by Winter's spies with that hair o' yourn? You should have been taken at the gates."

"I have many a resource," Ingamald patted her leather pouches.

"Ah. You paid them off then. Good wench!"

"Nay, no payment. Only secret knowing and a few tricks. I come to help. What is your name?"

"Ev. And yours?"

"Sall."

The woman eyed her. "To help is it? Well, we could use quite a bit o' that, I'll warrant."

"In exchange."

"For what?"

"I'll know it when I see it." Ingamald tied back her copper hair.

"Then I'll be wanting something, too. In exchange."

"In exchange for what?"

"Lettin' you in 'ere."

Ingamald was in no mood to quibble. "Name it then."

"A couple o' coppers to put on the eyes o' the dead."

Ingamald pulled out two coins from her skirt pocket. Ev snatched them away.

"Come you then...Sall, is't?" The elderly woman led her to a large chamber lit only by a great fireplace in which bubbled a cauldron full of watery broth. Strewn about were perhaps twenty pallets where numbers of men, women and children lay shivering and shuddering in disease. Crying out in distress. Moaning through their fevers.

"These 'ere 'gainst the north wall are coffin-ripe. They'll be dead soon enough. O' the ague. Don't know what it is you can do for them, if anything. These others lyin' about, well…Dunno what ails them. One guess is good as t'other. Everything from runny noses to arses. That there," Ev pointed across the way to a small wooden door, "is the pox room. I wouldn't advise you go in 'less you're lookin' to shake 'ands with death." And she shuffled off to assist another woman who was shrouding a body in the corner.

Ingamald threaded her way through the pallets, looking to help whomever she could. She reset the broken arm of a woman who had suffered a fall and had lived through a day and a night in pain. She fed several ailing children broth and water, found them coverlets dirty but warm to fend off the night chill. She cleansed and stitched open wounds, bandaging them with strips of her own petticoats. She brewed willow bark tea and helped the feverish to drink.

Finally, in the hour before dawn, she opened the door to the pox room. The stench greeting her was a noxious blend of rot and feces. Ingamald pulled her head from the door and knotted a rag securely about her nose and mouth. Grabbing a sconce from the wall, she reentered.

About her were the miserable remains of perhaps ten people barely living or already dead. Angry pustules mapped the skin of a woman near the door; she lay deathly still but for the rasping in her throat. Near her another stirred under a filthy rag. A hand reached out from behind Ingamald and clutched her boot. The witch half-screamed.

Nearby she found that which she sought. A child. Its ravaged face a frozen mask, open eyes staring straight up to the vaulted ceiling. A child dead three hour. Ingamald choked on the bile rising in her throat. But removed the quilt unflinchingly and thrust it in one of her two pouches. Gagging, she left the death room.

Left Ev and her helpmate robbing a dead man of his rings. Left the scene of suffering and sickness. Left behind the inn and its miserable inmates and hastened through dawn shadows back to the room where Ingo lay softly snoring.

The witch secured the one pouch with its dangerous contents on the ledge outside the window. She washed her hands again and again in the soapwort leaves from her other pouch, tossing the basin water out the window. Exhausted, Ingamald fell asleep at the table, her head buried in her weary arms.

The Troubadour threw the offending letter upon the brazier fire.

"So. Thinks the witch she can bar my entrance to Sprïggen?"

"Aye. That's wha' she said—you're not to come." Ingo's voice betrayed nothing as he looked at Lira, Erabesque and Yda seated about the Musica caravan. "Nor none 'o you either."

"Witch or no, alone she will be easy prey for the pale fiend. She'll be in his vile clutches before day is broken. I leave tonight. Now!" The Musica man reached for his greatcoat. He stood next to the hook that held his tack and riding gear.

Lira spoke up. "I did not travel sixteen days to be left behind. Yda and I have already tarried together a fortnight in wonder and fear."

"Brother, I come too." Erabesque's tone dared rebuke.

The Troubadour turned to her, spurs in hand. "No time, no place for…"

"For womenfolk?" Lira spoke with uncharacteristic sharpness.

He flashed her a gold smile. "I do not have to say since you have said."

"I thought we were united in solidarity against the tyrant." Lira persisted. "You never spoke such before in Ingamald's presence. No, nor would you dare. What misbegotten heart-tumult over Ingamald rouses you to speak in ignorance about what we women have to offer in this trial?"

A loud clash punctuated Lira's remark as spurs hit the caravan floor. "I, ignorant? No, rather sensible! What strength in women's arms? How well do you ride?"

"Well enough, brother! So! Now you alone," Erabesque's voice shook, "have the brute force to cross the moat, batter down the Sprïggen castle doors, penetrate her inner chambers, slit the despot's throat, and spring the dungeon locks to set a witch free? Arrogance!

"You forget that I hold the cards, dear brother. Where is your foreknowledge in all of this?" The Musica woman held aloft the Fortuna. "And lest you forget you, I need only take you to Maghenta, our mother, to remind you of your place in this family, next to mine, not above! And I say that women have much more might hidden in their pockets and undergarments than men like you can imagine!"

The Troubadour's lips were tight. "So. Stubborn is woman's will. So be it. But tell me, who will care for your son and Yda whilst you sneak about Sprïggen?"

"Well you know, brother. Husband Olan will as Olan does always. Yda is welcome ever in our caravan."

"Fie on that!" Yda will-bent the wall hook so surely that the gear and tack plunged to the floor, narrowly missing the Troubadour's head.

Ingo whistled. "I think the lass moight 'ave a trick or two to turn on old Morty. Let's not forget, she knows the dungeon better than any o' us, should Ingamald indeed be captured. Says I, Yda comes. Winter wanted her for somethin'. Never know, tha' could prove useful, too. Any way, she's safer in our care with eight eyes upon her."

The group looked from Yda to Ingo, and one by one nodded reluctant agreement.

"And as a wee matter o' interest, Eraybesque, I'd loik to know wha' them cards o' yours, say. What be our Winter prospects? Tell us, if you please."

The bickerers grew still. "I see ice and not much else. The Fortuna speak always lately of chillfrost."

"There's a thought to sober a drunkard." Ingo stood. "I left the witch asleep in me rooms. I daren't trust she'll stay there long. Now that it's nightfall, I'll warrant the cat's awake. Still, it's safer to travel by starry light. I say, let's take the Troubadour's lead and set out. We'll have to clamber o'er the city walls, but I knows a place where the wall's a bit crumbly. Then we'll to Ingo's rooms until our next move. Think on 'ow and wha' tha' moight be and save the grumblin' for later. Let's keep our wits about us and tempers in check."

The Troubadour picked up his spurs and tack.

"And Troubadour, it's best we go on foot. 'Orses will rouse the guards. And where will we store the beasts? Besoids, it's easier to approach in shadow and get ourselves in and o'er in short order. Take a little longer, but leastways we'll save our necks this one noight."

The Musica man examined the bent wall hook, and reset his riding gear against the wall. Erabesque flew off to inform her mother of the departure plan, while Yda and Lira donned warm clothing for the night journey.

Under a cold moon they turned their collective backs upon the warmth of the Musica encampment. They chose the road less travelled and ill-repaired to approach the walls of Sprïggen city. The wind rose as if to whip them backwards. Still the small group marched on. In three hours, the spires of the castle appeared in the moonlit distance, and the allies abandoned the road altogether for the fallow, snow-covered fields. Turning cruel, the wind veiled the moon with thick clouds.

Ingo tripped lightly over the hard bumps and clods of snow. The Troubadour and his sister, used to such terrain, stepped swift and sure. Yda stumbled in the darkness frequently as her small feet caught in the ruts and pits. Lira, also less than sure-footed, scrambled to help the child. They panted after the others, wind chafing their hands and cheeks. Shy of a league from the castle walls, as if to deter them from purpose, snow began to tumble from the sky, further obscuring their night vision. Headbent, the retinue pushed on.

Wary of the town watch, Ingo advised that each traveller should dart from brush to brush. Thus, stealthily, they crept nearer the walls. Once there, they flattened themselves against the brick and mortar as the snow picked up, blowing icily about their ears.

The night guard was changing shift. Halloos and hawking of the sentries reached their ears, but none detected their presence. Soon, all was quiet but for the footfalls of the lone sentinel as he patrolled the wall above their heads. On signal from Ingo, the group kept very still. Yda fought back her sniffles in the frigid air. Finally, the footsteps passed them by.

Relieved to again be moving, the group followed Ingo through the thick snowfall away from the direction of the guard's patrol. The fire-eater led them to the portion of the wall in disrepair. He leapt over nimbly then assisted the rest, the Troubadour giving a leg up to each on the other side. Second last to cross over was Lira. She and the Musica man eyed each other. Then he bowed slightly towards her, this small gesture enough to convince her to accept his offer of help. He followed close behind.

Once inside the walls of Winter's self-appointed city, the chilled quintet hurried through the darkened streets littered with carnival debris. The storm now worked to their advantage. No one was about this frigid night; shutters were closed against inclement weather. At last the group reached the portal to Ingo's room. He unlocked the two doors and bade his cold and weary companions enter.

As he had feared, Ingamald was gone.

She'd raised her tousled copper head from a cramped sleep at Ingo's table late that same afternoon. The weak winter sun was already shrinking behind the city walls. Ingamald helped herself to bread, cheese and the key left behind by her fire-eating friend. She assumed rightly that he was just about to deliver her letter to the Troubadour. Hope and doubt battled within over whether the Musica man would heed her words.

Ingamald braided her hair thoughtfully. This was a time apt for espial. In the fading light, she would seek the way to the castle and find the means to enter. She threw her green cloak about her shoulders, adjusting the mantle securely over her flaming hair. Before the looking glass, she affixed her cat-mask, then turned from her own emerald gaze. Pausing long enough at the window to retrieve the pouch and its sickly contents, she quitted Ingo's close chamber, locking the door behind her and setting a quick spell of security about the place.

Steeling herself, the witch stepped into the carnival fray. With an eye to the west where the sun was near setting, she wound her way through the narrow jostling streets of Sprïggen. Winter's castle, she knew now, lay southwest, separated from the city proper by a second walled partition. A lively bunch of merrymakers seemed headed that way. Indeed, they crossed into the public gardens of the castle. There colourful dissemblers and performers now gathered for nighttime festivities aside the very scaffolds and stakes of Winter's public trials and executions. Ahead lay the grand arch just before the moat of Winter's castle. The drawbridge would be down until midnight. When the first flints sparked to light the night torches, Ingamald peeled away from the crowds. A bush of holly against the ivy-covered arch offered prickly camouflage.

Sprïggen bells tolled the sixth hour. From her hiding place, the witch saw the flickering lights of the carnival revellers a-busy at their antics. Reassured that no one paid her heed, she crept on all fours from her sanctuary. Ingamald crossed underneath the arch. Any onlooker would have merely beheld a ginger cat slinking along the flagged roadway towards the drawbridge. Behind her, hidden amongst the holly and its berries, her single pouch, a pile of clothing and a discarded mask.

CHAPTER

CAT PAD OVER THE DRAWBRIDGE across the moat. Sure of sinew and paw. Slide about the open great gate and through the legs of the sentry.

"Scat cat!" Hurling pebble grazes fur between shoulder blades. Scamper up a tree to gaze greenly on foe below shaking fist. Climb further to certain safety. Ah, this oak is twinned; one half on either side of wall. Cat-wise to remember. Now the wall is a quick cat leap. Ledge is narrow but safer for catprowling.

Ahead the castle and an open window. A running feline vault atop the sill. A silent four-foot drop to flagstone floor. And inside the villain's castle. To violate the violator. Tit for tat. Kit-cat.

Where to Hana? Where to Morton Winter?

Cat curves through the corridors. Sniff of mould and must. Chill drafts of winter without and within. Dark corners where mousies hide. No time for hunting. Pad by the prey.

Wind up around a stairwell, another and another. Down another dimlit hallway. Cold stone with many spider webbings. Fight cat desire to swat at spider, to catmunch eight leggies.

Heavy door down the way flings suddenly open. Marching legs of liveried servants pass by, nearly cat-crushing. Dart between and through to doorway. Cat coil around the door and in. Exiting servile retinue continues. Now only a few persons remain within. A foul cold smell, metallic. It is the fiend's very quarters. Winter's inmost chamber.

Ingamald-cat first beholds him, seated silver on a dais. Morton Winter. Massive. Corpulent. White feathers for hair. Watery eyes. Pale, plump hands with sharpened nails. Snowwhite and crystal gemstones—on his clothing, around his neck, on his fingers. A silver throne, also gem-studded. In the far left corner, silver-draped like its owner, the magic table. Around the dais, beneath the cold master, cushions for attendants and sycophants. At his left, fool in motley. At his right, golden-haired Gretchen. Before him a dwarfish who speaks while cat eavesdrops:

"Master Winter, I ask that you consult your magic table on my behalf only once more. If there is no news of my son, Wenceslas, I will give him up for dead. I must quit this work and this place."

"And go where, Dagnott? Where are your people now? Others of your kind revile you. Where would you be safe, my dwarf?" Winter reached for a piece of sugared fruit.

"Aye, dwarf-folk hate the dastardly work I do for you, and so hate Dagnott, too. So I will away alone to live out my days."

"You mean drink them away, dwarf. No, I see more profitable work for you."

"What more can I do? I have completed your wretched device."

"You can help me catch and torture that witch and her comrades, that's what. And if you want to hear anything of Wenceslas—whether dead or living again—you will do my bidding. I hope your stunted head can understand that much. Now get you to your ale and drink yourself silly 'til the morrow when I will have need of you again!"

Dagnott swallowed a rumbling, volcanic rage. Helpless, hapless, he turned and left the great chamber.

Didion took his place before the pale lord. “No word of the witch Ingamald, Master Winter. And our spies tell us that her cottage is lost to them.”

“Burned to the ground it was.”

“No, Lord. Nearly so by all accounts. But now… no one in Bruë Wood can find a way to the charred ruin.”

“Magic!” Morton Winter slammed a beringed and furious fist upon the arm of his throne. “Make it known that when this Ingahag is caught, she will learn that my wrath has no bounds.”

“As you will it, Lord Winter.” Didion’s hunched back bowed low, and he moved away from the dais.

“And now our guest, Gretchen. How fare you this carnival eve, dear daughter of Rote?”

“As well as yestereve and all the yesterdays you have kept me hence imprisoned.” Gretchen glared at her despicable host.

“Ah. Well and good then. Your tower keep room offers a fair view of the carnival caperers. Retire you thence.” A lady-servant rose to guide Gretchen from Winter’s great apartment.

“Now Fool! Charm us with capricious entertainment fit for this blasted carnival season.”

The spry man in motley leapt to his feet. “Oh, I’ve a merry tale for you this e’en Lord Winter.”

“Say on, Fool, say on.”

“Well… here it is then. *The Ballad of the Boil:*

Once there was a merry time
When all was gay and trim
’Til sweet beheld and sweet indulged
That was the end of slim.

Now on a cool December day
He naked rose, alas
And there in perfect purple hue
A pimple on his…

Ask me no more questions
I ne'er have spoke a lie
This very lord in question
Could only wonder why.

He summoned forth the surgeon
Who scratched a balding pate
He summoned forth his ministers
Who stood with breath a-bate.

He sought the cure of laxative
The lord was so besot
But what was got of remedy?
A smelly chamber pot!

He'd murdered ev'ry herbalist
Each witch and healer, too
And as he moaned and wailed abed
The boil, it grew anew.

It waxed in purple size and hue
It pained him to the touch
It grew as like enough to burst
Chagrin, it brought him much.

At last he summoned forth his fool
A gentleman forsooth
Noble, aye and handsome too
Who ever spoke in truth:

'The case is clear to me, my lord,
At but a single glance,'
And taking aim with one sure hand,
He pricked the boil with lance.

Amid the lordly screams,
The fool proclaimed, 'Too much repast!
'Too many sweets, too many meats,
Gave birth to boil upon your

Ask me no more questions
I ne'er have spoke a lie
I live to tell this tale tonight
Tomorrow I might die!'

Shoe sails past feline ear. Flurry of retreating motley. Bells jingle by in hasty departure. Another shoe hits the rump of fool. Cat scurries to follow his jangling feet through the closing chamber door. Safely outside, jester and hunchback waiting walk together downwards. Ingacat slinks stealthily after.

Downwards through portals and corridors. Countless descending steps. Through doorways and under stone archways. Dimmer and dimmer the light.

And at last the vaults below the castle. A room with a single light. Seated at table, the dwarf, Dagnott, huge stein in hand. Blearily, he spies the puss peering. Hurls his ale mug at her ginger form, catluckily with poor aim. Furtive feline dart to catch up with fool and hunchback.

They turn into a long hall. At the end, a solid black door. The misshapen one turns a key in lock. Together, hunchback, fool and cat enter and are shut and locked within. A flint strikes. A torch is lit. All is gloom and mildew.

The men speak in hushed tones.

"That was a fine performance you dared, Fool."

"If you could have seen the colour rage into the colourless face!"

Their laughter hisses about the walls as they pass through. A black gaping chamber on the right. Catnose detects no one, but catssenses panic, distress, suffering. The smells of the place are enough even to sicken a tom. Four pussfeet pad hurriedly on.

A gate unlocks ahead. And sounds of human captives fill feline ears. Outcries and chains rattling. Some miserable rakes a tin cup against the bars, begs for water.

The hunchback speaks sharply to the guards who grumble after water for the thirsty.

Cat sniffs the malodorous air for scent of Hana. Where she? Where Hana? The fool and his lumpish friend step ahead. No time to search for Hana now. Cat springs after them.

Hunchback and jester proceed to the deadend wall of stones. A jingle and a push upon one stone, and the wall scrapes open. Quickly the two men and cat slip through, and the wall scrapes closed. Now two men plus one witchcat know the secret passage.

In darkness the men feel their way along the damp tunnel. Cat-eyes follow surely behind. A sound of a trapdoor and a flint. Feet ascending up a wooden ladder. Cat bounds up in pursuit. And the two catch sight of a fleet orange form diving deep under the bed.

One, the jangling jester, reaches for a broom to sweep out a cat. She hisses viciously at him, arching her back into the farthest corner. Japester and cat stare each at the other. Fool wisely abandons the attack.

Drops his motley. Draws on thick velvet. Dons spectacles. Peeping through the dustballs and shadow, witchcat finds the fool has turned alchemist.

"The pusscat will out when she wishes."

"Where did the moggy come from?" Didion pulled a chair up to the table cluttered with alchemic apparatus.

"Cats are creatures of mystery. Who knows? To matters more important, Didion. Have you really no word of Winter's enemies?"

Didion accepted a cup of hot tea his host offered. "None. They elude him and his agents. Prince Ranðulfr had the witch Ingamald in his keep and lost her, but I'll not risk his sister Gretchen's neck in telling the tyrant that bit of news. My suspicion is that the rebels are here in the city. Disguised for Carnival, they wait to work some insurrection during the public trials. Or executions."

"I'll warrant they have some grand mischief planned. More power to them." The alchemist raised his cup in salute.

"I fear none of them have long to live, Svalbaard."

A 'mirrow' startled the men. The alchemist looked again beneath the bed into the green eyes of his feline guest.

"Do I know you?" he mused aloud, then shrugging, returned to Didion. "I fear their fates, too, friend Didion. I fear for my d…"

Cat creeps cautious from beneath the bed. Didion springs towards her as if to catch. She leaps to a high shelf. Trapped. Fearful. The hunchback reaches for the broom. Catwitch hisses fiercely at his approach.

"Put down the broom, Didion."

"Eh? I thought…"

"Don't torment the creature. Here, pusscat. The door. Leave as you wish. Or stay." The alchemist unlocked the front door to his humble hut.

A ginger streak and catfree out the door. Out from the house on the hill beyond the castle walls. Cavorting downwards. Back through the snow and dark to the great arch before the castle moat. Back to where she started.

In human form, the witch snatched up the secreted pouch and crossed again through the arch. The hour was well past midnight; the drawbridge up. There was naught to do but swim the moat. Stifling a shriek, she plunged into the black, ice-chilled waters and struggled awkwardly across, keeping the satchel free of the water. She emerged trembling on the other shore. Slipping and scrambling, Ingamald pulled herself up the bank and crawled along in search of the twin tree. Her limbs grew numb with cold.

Cat-fierce, she climbs the tree and trots along the wall to the same still-open window. Clenched in teeth, the pouch.

Sure paws find the way anew to the hall of Morton Winter's chamber. All is still and silent now in the sleeping castle. A single sentry dozes before the locked door of Winter's private place.

Calming her cat-heart, she witch-wills an illusion.

Around the corner, towards the slumbering guard, strode Ingamald in Didion form. The sleeping man jolted awake and stood. In Didion-guise, with head averted, she nodded once, sharply.

The guard hesitated. Not daring to speak, Ingamald-as-Didion turned a hideous visage, with protruding eye and tongue, fully upon the attendant. He blanched suddenly and snatched up the key to open the door.

She entered and the lock slipped behind her.

In a massive, ornate bed a behemoth form snored soundly. The witch muttered a quickspell to keep him so, then crept past and over to the fabled Tabula, drawing its cover off with barely a whisper.

Placing damp hands upon her black face, Ingamald mind-spoke to Tabula.

"I am called Ingamald."

"I know." A dream voice resounded in Ingamald's thoughts. The only noise in the chamber was the crackling of logs in the great fireplace.

"What are you?"

"A speaking stone. The Winter calls me Tabula."

"Are you his possession then?"

"Speaking stones belong to the earth, our mother. No man, no person is master."

"Why then do his bidding?"

"I do not. I show or tell what I will."

"The earth is my mother also. What stories can you tell me?"

In the centre of the black table, Tabula projected a curious tale while narrating:

"On a frigid evening in the miserable hamlet of Ut, a woman gives up a final grunt and her ghost in giving birth to a seventh son. Morton, last and least of the line of Winter men, and worse, an albino.

"Resentful of her early departure from life, he feels her absence as a personal injury. A child who grows fitfully, sickly and thin from the outset, Morton's frequent and varied illnesses persist throughout his youth and into manhood. By turns moribund and irascible, Morton Winter is a child wanting.

"Infirm of mind he is not. Clever with words, sharp of tongue, he early decides that his six brothers and distant father are lumpish oafs, undeserving of his attention. And so he turns it elsewhere. He likes to thieve and finds he has a talent for it, training his deft white fingers to pocket and secret away objects of his desire: apples, sweets, daggers. Of these latter, he grows especially fond, delighting in their metallic sheen and edges so like his own: piercing and keen. Over the years he amasses an impressive collection of weaponry until, discovering thumbscrews and stakes, his tastes turn to torture. He briefly entertains an aspiration to hire out as county hangman.

"A young lad of fifteen, he leaves home with narry a backwards glance. Never again does he see kith or kin. Because of his infirmity, Morton cares little for the sun and so turns away from it, preferring colder climes and people. He seeks the employ of wealthy men, especially those who are owed money, and wins notoriety as a debt collector. Small and frail, he seldom employs his methods directly, more often relying on brutish hirelings who, at his behest, apply heat or club to flesh or kneecap. His professional services are widely sought after.

"By thirty years, Morton Winter has acquired a tidy fortune, some of which he uses to purchase the town and lands of Sprïggen. Here he erects this fortress, surrounding himself with sycophants and dilettantes, while setting peasants and serfs to work his lands. He fears those with knowledge and grows mistrustful of any who read, finally forbidding his own subjects any schooling. Eventually, as his lands and power expand, he outlaws books entirely.

"His dalliances tilt towards the deviant. He prefers the company of stolen women, girls and boys. And always, his fondness for metal instruments inform his play. Often he seeks the pleasure of some drug or distilled liquour to enhance his leisure.

"Once he loves. A green-eyed woman taken captive. In her eyes he beholds a beloved reflection. Entirely enamoured, he offers her his wealth, his power if only she will give herself. She will not. And so she dies. Beheaded by a Kintish sword and swordsman. Afterwards, Morton Winter keeps her embalmed left pinkie finger as a sentimental token.

"Since the woman, Morton Winter's affections are solely reserved for possession. Jewels, adornments, instruments of truth extraction. And his most prized, the table on which your hands rest, some claim is magic, others that it merely casts Winter's own black reflection. What he little knows is that he, the Winter, is a man truly possessed.

"Some nights the lone man weeps piteously for hours, until liquor or sleep or both consume him."

Ingamald replied silently to the stone, "Should I then pity this man? This bloated version of a boy ill-raised and ill-loved?"

"I do not instruct."

"Do you know the future?"

"Nay. I see what is and what was."

"Why did you tell Morton Winter about us?"

"I do not know why. I do not always tell him what he wills to know."

The witch considered. "Where do you belong?"

"Wherever I am."

"You have no home where you would rather?"

"Wherever I am, the earth is."

"You do not care about the ill this man wreaks?"

"I neither fear nor care. I merely am."

Ingamald looked deeply into Tabula's blackness. "What more, then, can you tell me?"

"I know that your companions are come to Sprïggen."

The witch sighed and shook her head resignedly. "As I feared."

"They are safe tonight."

"Do not tell Morton Winter their whereabouts."

"I may. I may not." Tabula's voice in the wiccan mind was expressionless. Ingamald briefly considered what she could offer such a stone to forge an alliance, then abandoned the idea as futile.

"What further can you show me?"

Images began to flicker across the obsidian face. Ingamald was transported to the tower keep where Gretchen slept, attended by her lady-servant. A flicker and the scene changed to a small boy, a dwarf child also slumbering and likewise attended.

"Who is the child?"

Tabula did not answer.

But by the next breath, Ingamald knew. "The dwarf's son! Dagnott's missing child, Wenceslas! He is kept prisoner unbeknownst to the father. Thus is the father kept choked on a chain."

Tabula's face went blank.

"Speaking Stone… what know you of the witch Hana?"

At first, Ingamald despaired that the stone would reveal aught of her beloved foster mother and mentor. Then a quick series of pictures flashed by to tell the awful tale. First Hana's capture by mounted men, just after the old witch stepped beyond the safety of her stone circle in Hören Wood. Flash to a chamber, the dark unlit one, Ingamald had earlier passed in catform. Therein, a fist to an eye. Another to her back. A kick to her mouth. Followed by several wretched, dank nights in a dungeon cell. Deprivation. Near starvation. A visitor. A vial. A dawn's drinking of the contents.

Next the scene flitted to Hana's final moments. Ingamald caught a fleeting glimpse of Winter's instruments of torture. A draped instrument, no doubt most horrid, nearby. And then, Hana's collapse.

Ingamald half-sobbed, but froze at the desecration that followed.

The image moved to a stake and smoking bier upon which a masked brute secured the corpse-that-was-Hana. Then a final glimpse of the aged body consumed by flame as ugly bystanders ranted and jeered.

Ingamald pulled her hands from the stone and buried her face. She bit her knuckles to keep from screaming rage. Pain. Loneliness and utter aloneness. That Hana would meet such an ignominious end. That Ingamald, supposed to be so powerful, Hana's apt pupil, was finally, so absolutely powerless. Unable to save her. Unable.

Well, she was able enough now. At this moment. She left Tabula. Picked up the pouch. Walked witch-sure over to the bed of witless Winter. Gazed at his engorged, albinotic face.

And hated as she had never before. The impulse thrilled through her, boiling her blood. A drum pounded at her temple, urging her on to this deed for which she had planned. She imagined placing the pox-coverlet ever-gently o'er his brow, and leaving quiet as her catself.

The drum thrummed onward as she thought of the fever and cramp that would confront the villain next day. A blistering of the skin by nightfall. Through the discontent of twelve hours the blisters would become pustules, puss-filled and throbbing. Neither food nor water would his weakened body accept. Winter would drift between hot and cold, delirium and waking, monstrous nightmare and feverish hope. Pustules would begin to close his throat, rasp his breathing. His skin would feel tautly afire, but if he touched or worse, scratched, the boils would break and the pain would increase tenfold.

Her temple drummed towards crescendo. So would Winter exist a night and a day more perhaps, at best. In the end, screams for help would turn to raving to whimpers to rasping, aching, writhing, death.

Then they would burn his body. Publicly. Humiliatingly. Just as he had done Hana's. Her wiccan daughter would see to it personally.

Ingamald smiled in satisfaction at these secret witch-thoughts. Her fingers fumbled with the pouch buckle. Her heart pounded in time with the crashing drum.

Hana's voice came to her. "Would you use wicca for ill?"

Ingamald shook her head. This was no ill-use, but good-use. To end the tyrant's reign was right. Return Hinterlünd to its former self. Good. Healthy. She would use sickness to procure health.

The witch-woman steadied herself. Her hand reached inside the pouch for the soiled sickcloth. Her drumming heart was deafening.

Hana's influence persisted. "Sickness to procure health? The pox to peace? When has the pox ever claimed but one?"

Her fist clenched as the young witch foresaw.

First the servants, ignorant of her sick plan, would come on the morrow to rouse the master. And in touching him be likewise contaminated. They would carry the pestilence with them. Back to their quarters. Or worse, out in the streets to spew the pox throughout the carnival. As word of Winter's disease spread—and it would as surely as the pox itself—terrified visitors and revellers would quit the city in each direction of the wind. And like the wind, the plague would spread. Who in Hinterlünd would be safe, except the very lucky? And who but a single, vengeful witch would be responsible for the epidemic?

She looked at the repulsive form before her. An accursed man she wished to curse with a most malingering death.

Had he killed Hana, this tyrant? Hana gave herself up. Took her own life with a dram of poison. What breed of witch, what worthy practitioner of wicca would do as Ingamald planned?

"There must be justice!" Tears began to cloud her vision. Her temple, like her clenched hand still inside the leather pouch, pulsed painfully.

A small, knowing voice calmed her. "Justice, yes, for the others imprisoned, oppressed, tortured and burned. Swift justice for them. But not this way. Not this time. Not at peril to all innocent living in Hinterlünd." Her fist relaxed, surrendered. The thudding rhythm slackened.

Ingamald gagged on self-repugnance. At her ill-conceived plan to breed contagion.

She pulled her fingers swiftly out of the pouch. Dismayed by her own malice, dazed by perplexing thoughts, she withdrew, backing away from Winter's bed. In haste, the witch tossed the pouch, contents and all, upon the significant fire in Winter's chamber. Over her retreating shoulder, a whispered incantation for peptic distemper, directed towards the dreamer. Dawn would find him retching into his chamber pot.

A spell on the lock and it was sprung. Hurriedly, before she could change her uneasy, whirling mind, she staggered hunchbacked from the chamber, past the surprised guard.

Two turns down empty corridors and hunchback *shrugs to feline form skitting down many stone stairwells, out the courtyard window, dashing through falling snow to the twin trees near the wall. Catclaw up tree and over wall down the sister tree to the steep edge of the moat. Twisting free to* human witch form, Ingamald swam fiercely across the murky, frigid waters. She pulled up numbly across the way and streaked through the snow, then the archway to the holly hiding place. There she retrieved her homespun and cloak and dashed half-frozen through the nightstreets back to Ingo's haven.

CHAPTER

INGAMALD AND HER INSURGENTS plotted for three days. For three days, Morton Winter suspended public trials and executions while he recovered from his stomach ailment. On the final day of carnival, these would resume. But by then, the connivers' scheme would be—with luck—well-conjured.

Quarters were close and more than once the dissemblers argued and tempers rose. On the third morning, irritated at the wrangling of wills, Lira slipped out into the carnival thoroughfare and the chill air. She wandered, masked and miffed, without real aim. Considering that someone needed to look to evening repast, she turned into the marketplace in search of supper provisions. As Lira haggled over the price of a slab of salted meat, she caught sight of an aged woman beckoning her. The Bookewoman! Here in Sprïggen! Trying to remain calm, she paid what the vendor asked and turned brusquely in the direction of the Learned crone.

"Well, met then, sister Lira. I've been a lookin' fer ye."

"It'll be death to you, mother, if Winter's spies find you out."

The aged one cackled. "Ha! It's sure he's seen me then through that great peepin' stone o' his. But come 'ere, then lass. Make like ye're lookin' at the merchandise."

Lira peered into the open cart before her. Bolts of cloth in many hues for sale. She rubbed a cotton swatch between her fingers. "Why, you've changed professions then?"

"Aye. Today, in these streets it's cottons and linens. As far as anyone knows. But if ye've a crafty eye, ye'll see the bookes beneath the bolts. Just a quick trap door, and all's hidden."

"What risk you take!"

The Bookewoman's crinkled face sobered. "These be risky times. I've come fer a reason, that's sure." With a crook'd arthritic finger she brought Lira's ear close to her toothless mouth. "I've twae messages. One fer the witch. One fer the hunchback. And sure enough, lass. Ye're my deliverer."

"I can bring a message to the witch. But I know of no hunchback. Unless you mean the one who lives in the icefoe's castle. Winter's own minister."

"Aye, lass. That's the very one. Didion, 'e's called."

"But he's a puppet to his master."

"Ach! Don't be deceived. Especially by the cover of a booke. I thought ye knew that much at least, Lira."

"I do, I…"

"Listen," the Bookewoman's voice hushed. "Take this to the witch." She handed Lira a sealed scroll. "And this," she pressed another to the young woman's breast, "to the hunchback. Fail me not, ye hear?"

"I… I will not fail."

"Goode! I'm glad to hear it. Get ye gone now." And in a sudden creaking the bolts of fabric folded inward, the open cart closed, and the Bookewoman wheeled away her barrow down the narrow market street.

"When next will I see you?"

Lira's query was answered with a burst of croaking laughter. "Ye're a silly, that's what! Why, when I've need o' ye, lambkin. Now, watch yer corners, instead of me rump!"

Lira tripped back to Ingo's room and burst in on the group. She told them what had transpired in the market and handed the first scroll to Ingamald. The witch unfurled it carefully. Her brow furrowed in concentration.

"Well, tell us, Witch!" Ingo blurted. "What does it say?"

"It is a puzzle."

"Yda is good at puzzles and tricks." The youngster tried to read over the witch's shoulder.

Ingamald read aloud: "It says, 'Look through the glass. Remember the twelve.'"

"And that is all?" The Troubadour was impatient.

"Aye." Lost in thought, Ingamald passed the scroll through the candle and set it aflame.

"Well, what does the other scroll read?" Erabesque demanded.

"That is for only one to know." Lira turned a willful face upon her co-conspirators. "Didion, the hunchback."

A rousing song from the street below broke the silence.

"Then, Lira," Ingamald tossed the ash of the burned scroll out the window and turned to her Learned friend, "let us posthaste to Winter's castle."

Amid protests, the two women left the party. They wound their way to the public gardens just before the great archway ahead of the moat.

"Here, I must go my own way and you yours," the witch told Lira. "Let us plan to meet again within the hour. If something untoward should happen, the other is to tarry no more than a quarter hour, then speed back to Ingo and the others."

Lira swallowed her misgivings and passed through the arch, over the drawbridge.

"I would speak with Didion," she told the guard firmly.

The ruffian eyed her hair and comely face. "Ha. Would you now? Didion has more important things to do than speak to a woman." The sentry laughed coarsely. "Besides. Pretty thing like you will faint dead away with one glimpse at him."

"Tell him that I have news about the witch Ingamald and her companions."

At this the guard sobered and whispered something to another watchkeep who scuttled quickly into the castle. Lira stood stonily before the lout, refusing to meet his eye. Within moments, the other returned and bade her enter.

Lira was brought first into the great courtyard, then into the grand hall of the castle proper. A man in livery led her to a smaller chamber, sparsely furnished but firelit and hung with rich tapestries. She waited, warming her hands the while. Moments seemed centuries. Trying to recall what she knew from Ingamald of the man, Didion, she braced herself for his ungainly entrance.

The door opened, admitting a hooded, bent figure. He turned his hunched back to her and spoke. His voice, Lira noticed, was gentle as a hummingbird's wings.

"I am Didion."

"Then I have a message for you."

"Who are you?"

"Lira."

"I mean, who *are* you?"

She looked at his back but wanted to see his face. How could she otherwise trust? Yet the Bookewoman had cautioned not to judge. Certain, the man was misformed, shrunken from his infirmity. Had he stood tall he would have been nearly six feet. All Lira knew to guide her was the tone of his voice. "Do you read, Didion?"

The hunchback raised his head at her question. "Yes." He swallowed audibly. "I read."

"As do I. I am a Learned. And I risk much in the telling of that."

"Indeed."

"Turn to me, Didion."

"I… I cannot."

"Wherefore?"

"I am hideous."

"The woman who gave me your message thinks not. Nor will I."

"Woman?"

"The Bookewoman."

The hunchback started. "I thought she was dead."

"I, too, feared so. But she lives. How came you to know her?"

A bell chimed in a castle tower. Midday. Lira was quietly patient.

"She… the Bookewoman is my mother."

Lira spoke gently but sure, "Turn, then, and meet a friend, Didion."

"I am afraid…"

"I am afraid, also. But not of you. Didion."

Slowly the hunched form shuffled about to her. Still he did not raise his face to her.

"Look at me. I am Lira."

With wrecked face, Didion at last looked upon her. His eyes were malformed, one drooping low upon his left cheek. A nose, misshapen perhaps from a beating, sat crookedly in the middle of his face. Fleshy wet lips pulled back in a grimace, revealed protruding teeth. His ears were of two sizes and shapes, and his hair was a thick thornbush atop his head.

Lira did not move, did not betray her revulsion. "You see. I am not turned to stone by you, Didion."

The grimace relaxed into a sort of smile, softening the grotesqueness, if only slightly. "That is the lore of trolls, not hunchbacks."

She smiled back at the man. "My mistake, then." From beneath her bodice, Lira produced the scroll. "Here, Didion. Your mother's message."

He accepted the offering. “Is she safely away? Where last did you see her? But no. Tell me not. Morton Winter will extract the knowledge, and she will be apprehended.” Didion unrolled the scroll and read. Lira turned to leave. “Do you not wish to know the contents?”

“The words are not for me, unless you will to share.”

“Mother writes, ‘My son, trust this messenger.’”

“And that is all?” Lira raised an eyebrow.

“Unless you have more to share.”

“I am with the witch. That is all I can tell. I know about the stone. If Winter sees this meeting in her face, tell him… tell him…”

“I will tell him you are an informant come to warn of a plot.”

“As you see fit, Didion.”

“It is the truth, more or less.”

“I must leave you.” Lira reached for the door handle.

“Thank you for this message. For news of the Bookewoman. For looking on me without fear.”

“You are most welcome…”

“You are the first…the first woman besides my mother…to do so.”

“May I then see you again in happier times, Didion.”

His hummingbird voice grew distraught. “There will be no happier times. Your friends will be caught, Lira. Morton Winter is most sure. And I regret, so am I.”

“Be then reassured. We do not underestimate the menace.”

The hunchback’s heart was as heavy as the slamming door.

Ancient bottles sat crusted with debris. Others filled with inky liquids littered a shelf. Out of a glass cylinder, a collection of eyes bore into her own two, staring greenly. A bubbling reached her ears. Ingamald examined closely the intricate apparatus of tubes and vials filled with boiling liquid.

"Is this how one turns lead to gold?" she asked the alchemist.

"You want me to reveal my secrets before you tell your own, then? You, who burst in from nowhere with scarcely a 'by your leave,' expect me to admit you into my confidence. What e'er do you take me for?"

The witch tossed her copper hair. "A fool. And an alchemist. That's what. I've no time for niceties. I need your trust. So I'll tell you. We met two evenings hence."

Svalbaard stared deeply into Ingamald's green eyes. "Ah, yes. If I'm not mistaken, I mistook you for a kitten."

"Aye. I heard you then speak to the hunchback. You bear Winter little goodwill."

"True enough… If he finds you, your life will be forfeit."

"He will not find me!"

"Winter has a stone."

Ingamald hissed. "You try my patience! I know the stone. I have spoken with her. Moreover, I have placed a spell of concealment about your hovel for the next hour, so your sanctuary is safe enough whilst we parley."

"You are the witch. Ingamald."

"Aye."

"Terrible tales are told about you…"

The witch shrugged.

"That you devoured your mother."

Ingamald looked at him squarely. "Are you afraid, alchemist?"

He met her eyes. "You did what needed doing. Your mother was venomous. She poisoned me."

"What say you?"

The alchemist hesitated. "You may think me foolish," he began quietly, "but I am also Svalbaard, your once-wizard father. Spinne and I…"

A stunned Ingamald sat down upon the nearest stool. Father and daughter regarded each other. She saw little in him that bore resemblance to herself. But then Ingamald never forgot that she was her mother's daughter. The mother who had poisoned this man, her mate, and left him to die. A former wizard of the Congress of the Light now a fool in Winter's court. But also an alchemist, a trade for which she had considerable wiccan respect.

Svalbaard, in turn, saw a fiery young woman, quick to passion. Not one to suffer fools gladly. He smiled in admiration at this daughter he had never known.

When the witch spoke again, she did so with kinder intent. "Svalbaard, I thought you were blind and lost."

"I was. And now found and a fool."

"And an alchemist. Turning dross to gold for a cold fiend?"

"Ingamald, hear my story." In brief, the alchemist told of his indebtment to his master, then listened to his daughter's tale of Spinne's defeat, of Ingamald's part in the events leading up to Winter.

"You are, as they foretold, a great power, my daughter."

"I could not save Hana..."

"That matters not."

"That is all that matters. A great witch would save another."

"Perchance Hana saw in her own waning life your best chance."

"Svalbaard," Ingamald could not bring herself to call this man 'father.' "I need your help. I need this, your humble house. I need the secret passage. When you are gone to play the fool this eve, give me leave to enter this place."

"Granted. But why?"

Her green gaze met his. "Best you should not know."

"Keep your secret then, daughter. But here's one of mine I give to you." Adjusting his spectacles, the alchemist pored over a shelf of books, finally selecting a dusty volume. This he opened carefully, turning pages until he reached the leaf he desired.

Svalbaard handed her the page to peruse, then moved to a locked cabinet set in the wall. From its shelves, he chose a greenish long-necked bottle, and brought it over to her.

"This is the potion I have long laboured over. I have only to pour it into this ring, you see." The alchemist held before her a ring in the design of a dragon which curled about his finger. Five upraised talons clutched what appeared to be a moonstone gem—actually a concealed chamber for the dram—the other five clawed the air. It was a beautiful figure, fine-crafted in silver. Exquisite. Lethal.

Svalbaard poured liquid from the bottle into the moonstone chamber. Ingamald turned her attention back to the text. Her finger paused at the list of ingredients on the page. "The main ingredient is milk of poppy. For whom is this ring intended?"

"Now it is a gift, daughter, for you."

On close inspection the witch saw that the upturned talons, designed to puncture flesh, were the means by which the potion was to be administered.

"What would you have me do with this, Svalbaard?"

"Use it for your protection or…"

"Or mine own end."

The alchemist nodded.

"If you have alchemic means to work my end, then you most surely have the means to work Winter's end. Why have you yourself hesitated to do the deed?"

"Hana asked the same question."

"You spoke with her?"

"The night before she died."

Witch turned to fool. "You gave her the vial that took her life before the tyrant could. And now you pass a similar potion to me."

Again Svalbaard nodded. And Ingamald recognized a man who had indeed been ruined by her mother's sting. In his small world, the once-magician had grown fearful and inert. Afraid to act; afraid to risk. His life, she saw, was a kind of death. As in the past, the witch swore to be beholden to no man, no one. Whatever the cost. Her own life, if need be. For any mage, wizard, witch to be thus yoked by another's power was nevermore truly powerful. She placed the ring on the third finger of her left hand. It fit snugly. The witch admired the stone thoughtfully.

"Tell me, Alchemist. Do you have any other stones of legend? Certain pebbles that cast a light in the dark?"

Svalbaard brightened. "Ah, you mean *fosfor*. Indeed, I have some such of my own making." He leapt to his cupboard and produced a small velvet purse. Opening the pullstring mouth, Svalbaard poured a handful of its contents—tiny stones, pearlescent in the dim cottage light—into Ingamald's palm.

"Pebbles treated with urine cooked over red heat."

"These will gleam and glow, even in darkness?"

"Even so, daughter."

Ingamald returned the glimmering pebbles to their pouch and secured it beneath her cloak.

"I thank you for your gifts, Svalbaard."

The father looked softly into the young face. "I never dreamt to see you, Ingamald, until Hana told me my daughter lived. Now I would you'd run from this place, from Winter, and live on. The wan villain is bent on your destruction and you were best removed…"

"So fools e'er speak folly. This place, this time is where I am best, Svalbaard." Ingamald pulled her cloak over her hair, affixing her mask. The alchemist followed her to the door.

"Good was borne of Spinne and me."

"Aye. Let us remain hopeful of that, Svalbaard." And the witch's quick exit sent a chill up the fool's spine.

A circle of friends, they sat together. Candles flickered about Ingo's room.

Erabesque read the cards laid out in a symmetrical pattern before her. "A Fool in reverse betides chaos. An upsidedown Mage presages bungling. Reversed scales bode delay and deterrence."

She sighed, turning more cards from her pack. "Here are we all. Queens—brunette, fair, and dark denote Yda, Lira and myself—all topsy turned turvy. A knave with a sword—Ingo; a knight with a sword—the Troubadour. Again reversed. Only one is righted: the High Sorceress. So. Ingamald. Still, with this pattern, all that your card portends are secrets hidden."

Frowning, Erasbeque dealt the final cards. "Cups overturned. Contents spilled and frozen. Emptiness. Loss. A cold time. And finally…the World turned on its side. Ayi!"

"Peace, Erabesque." Ingamald touched her friend's shoulder. "The cards tell what already we know. Hinterlünd and all her peoples are in bedlam. Now is a coldly confusing time."

"Winter." The Troubadour next the witch, scowled darkly.

"But after winter comes spring." Yda's treble voice was hopeful.

"Aye. Tha's my way o' thinkin', lass." Ingo sat, cross-legged beside the girl. He gave Yda a wink.

"Let us review, friends." Ingamald filled a goblet with spiced wine and passed it around the circle. "Tonight we masked rabblerousers traverse the streets of Sprïggen. Make your way to the fool's house on the hill. There gain entrance to the underground passage by the means I've told. Drop these stones as you pass to light the way hither and to along the dark tunnel under the hill."

Ingamald held up a fosfor pebble, then passed the pouch to Yda.

"Inside the castle dungeons, your aim is to ferret out the prisoners. Lira, find you the hunchback and take him into your confidence. He is to present Ingo and Erabesque to the guards as Winter-sent entertainment for a hitherto cheerless Carnival eve.

"Ingo will create a flaming distraction to permit the Troubadour, Lira and Yda access to the dungeon corridors. Erabesque will, through charm and dance and drink, further beguile the guards, luring them early to drunken slumber. Then will Yda lead you to the prisoners' cells. If locks cannot be picked or sprung, no doubt Yda's quick fingers can find the ring of keys from some snoring sentry.

"Set free the wretched. Guide them through the passages back towards the alchemist's secret way. Remember, if the wall be closed, press the seventh stone, seven up and seven across.

"Get you quickly inside the house and quickly masked. Through the madness of the carnival streets make your way to the ill-repaired wall. Leave Sprïggen as you came. Get you back to the Musica camp.

"For my part, I will to the tower to free Gretchen and a young boy held captive there."

"And then you join us, witch?" Ingo lowered the cup, passed it to his left.

"Nay. I have another task. I must face Winter."

"So. This part of the plot you have not shared." The Troubadour faced Ingamald squarely. "Already, I do not like the strains of this coda."

"Troubadour, this meeting is solely my occupation. And you have always known so."

The Musica man did not answer but drank deeply from the goblet in his hand. He passed it to the witch.

She smiled around the circle. "You are a brave lot. I salute your friendship. Your courage." And she swallowed the final drops.

"Rest now a few hours until the frenzy reaches it peak. Then don we our gay apparel, and off to the tyrant's castle."

The company complied, stretching out and reclining where room permitted. But the Troubadour left abruptly. Ingamald found him in a sulk, sitting at the top of the stairwell. She squeezed beside him.

He spoke tersely. "We have come far, you and I."

"Aye." Ingamald smiled.

"To be now separated seems unfair."

"We have been parted afore and reunited. Many times."

"I no longer care for parting ways with you, witch."

She brushed a stray lock of hair from his eyes. "I want you safely away from here, Troubadour."

"I could stay and aid you. It is my deepest wish."

Ingamald shook her head.

"How can I leave you thus imperiled?"

"If you love Ingamald, you can and will."

"Ah, witch. And when will I know you love me?"

"When have you doubted?"

"Always."

"Do not then." And with her witch's forefinger she traced the sign of infinity upon his back.

Bedecked in pageant finery, the interlopers stepped out. Ingamald in her former cat mask and Ingo with his moonface. At their hips each carried a sack of disguises to abet the soon-to-be liberated. The Troubadour wore a wolfish grin. Erabesque an exotic bird beak. Lira walked as an aged crone and Yda as an impish sprite. They eased into the carnival cavalcade, cavorting through the streets without notice.

High-spirited merrymakers clamoured alongside them. Smells, pleasant and foul, reached their noses. Music regaled them through the streets. Passing the market, they saw a troupe of colourful acrobats flip lithely across the square. Cheers and applause rang out. Though the air was chill, the party of imposters were kept close and too warm.

Ingamald led her friends by a chain of hands held, through the crowds to the castle. Guards patrolled the drawbridge. Ingo created a diversion with a series of firesparks, as the witch led her troupe around the castle walls. At the foot of the fool's hill, they paused, collecting their breath and wits.

The witch embraced each fondly. "Be safe! Good fortune! And you, Troubadour," she took his face into her hands, "a witch-kiss for luck!" Then turning on her heel to the left, she left the company to trudge up the incline towards the alchemist's hilltop home.

Fleetfooted, Ingamald reached the holly bush. In a whisker's twitch, she switched to her catself and crossed through the arch and over the drawbridge, cat-shying past the sentries. By the time she gained the top of the castle wall, she spied the last of her friends enter the alchemist's abode. With a twitch of tail, she scampered into the open window of Winter's palace.

CHAPTER

THE STRONG OAKEN DOOR CRASHED OPEN, broken at the hinges. Two women within screamed.

"Gretchen!" A voice commanded from the hallway shadows. "Follow the ginger cat. And you, serving-woman!" The voice grew menacing. "Quit this chamber before the morrow and forfeit your life, hear you?"

Gretchen, pale but lovely, stepped into the tower corridor and trailed the darting orange tabby. They entered the spiral stairwell and began their descent.

"You who spoke…" the princess quavered. "Where are… Who… who are you?"

"It is Ingamald." The witch's name reverberated around Gretchen's head.

"Ingamald," Gretchen whispered, remembering the wiccan girl who'd waked her brother Ranðulfr with a kiss.

They entered a small passage, stopping before another door. As before, it too burst inward. The witch's imperative was repeated, this time directed towards the child and his guardian within. Small footfalls crept cautiously.

"Be not afraid, child." Gretchen urged the tiny boy. "Come hither. You are freed." He stepped into the narrow passage and the princess took his hand. "This cat… and I will guide you to safety."

Downwards, dizzily they spun. Only the occasional tower window offered any light for their retreat. At last they reached the bottom of the stairwell. Together, cat-burgler, princess and dwarf-child ran through empty castle corridors towards the small open window. Captives and cat squeezed through the opening and skirted along the castle wall to the twinned oak. The threesome scurried down the tree to the outside of the castle wall.

Shuddering, Ingamald resumed her true nature before the amazed eyes of her charges.

"Gretchen," the witch spoke in whispered haste, "this is Wenceslas, son of the dwarf, Dagnott. He must be kept safe. Where is Lord Field tonight?"

"At the Boar's Head Inn where he has waited these three weeks in vain. From there has he applied daily for my release from Winter's cold tower."

"Hie you thither with this child. Then get you three away and out of Sprïggen before the midnight locking of the city gates. Flee to Lord Field's home and not your own. There you will be safest. And keep the child from harm, Gretchen. Give me your word!"

"You have it and my love, too, Ingamald," the princess sobbed, hugging the witch.

"Do not, Gretchen, go to your brother. He is frozen in Winter's icy design. Go to Field's people."

"Aye, Ingamald."

"And you, Wenceslas," the wicca woman took hold of the small boy's shoulders. "I know you are bewildered and frightened by this night's confusion. But trust that you will see your father again. Trust this great lady. Trust me."

The dwarf-child's bright eyes brimmed with tears. He nodded once.

"Now, we three must swim this icy moat. On the other side, you will find a holly bush near the gate before the castle. Search among the leaves and find a bag with dry cloaks and carnival masks. Once disguised, make your way through the festival crowds to safety. Quickly now! Swim!"

And by example, she dived into the freezing moat waters. Princess and dwarfling did likewise. Gretchen swam well, but both women had to help the child in crossing. Deeply chilled, they dragged themselves up the opposite bank.

"Here I must leave you. Goodspeed!" And with a quickflash, the shivering witch switched to orange tabby, bounding off towards the nearby hill.

Just before the door of the alchemist's rude cottage, Ingamald turned woman again. Shivering, she lifted the latch and entered. Her father's dark cloak hung on a peg. She slipped into its velvet folds and tried to warm herself before the dying flames in the fireplace.

An hour passed. And another. The witch grew steadily anxious. She began to pace.

All had seemingly gone so well.

The would-be liberators entered the alchemist's cottage and discovered the trap-door with its ladder descending into the secret tunnel. Discarding their masks for the meantime, they stepped downwards into the musky underground. As they traversed the dank passage, Yda carefully left her pebbled trail of luminescence. By degrees they made their way at last to the closed wall.

Yda's quick fingers found the seventh stone. She pushed. The wall scraped open. And there, awaiting them on the other side, a battery of Winter's armed guards!

With weapons pointed surely at their throats, Erabesque, Lira and Ingo surrendered instantly. As the Troubadour scuffled with a guard, Yda dodged beneath their legs and managed to push again the seventh stone. The wall groaned closed as a second brute caught the child, screeching and pummeling his back, under his arm.

"So, Didion. These are they?" Morton Winter manuevered his massive girth about the bound and gagged prisoners before the great dais. He observed each closely. "I am wakened deep in the night for these? Scoundrels and vagabonds. Whoresons and rogues. Strumpets and filth-wenches. Those who stole from me…" He eyed Lira closely. "And, I see, some of my pilfered goods returned."

The pallid lord paused before a hooded form. Didion cleared his throat.

"The child, Lord Winter. With the twelve fingers and dread talent. She has been a-bending things."

"Things?"

"Swords. Lances. Keys in locks. We felt it best to keep her hooded."

"Yes. It is a talent we will harness for our own desires. Our best uses." He patted plumply Yda's covered head.

She struggled in her binds and, in her muffled voice, cried out, "Ingamald will get the frosty he! Aye, that the 'she' will!"

"Pardon, little one? Didion, unhood the child."

The hunchback lifted the sack from Yda's head.

"Say again," Winter coaxed.

Lira stamped her foot loudly. Yda shot the Learned woman a glance and kept mum.

"Sooo." Morton Winter smiled coolly into Yda's face. "Ingamald the wicked witch is friend to you…" he eyed the others craftily, "and yours. It is as I expected. And hoped. But no sign of this witch yet, Didion?"

"No, Lord Winter. She eludes capture."

Morton Winter sniffed twice. "Where then is the blasted alchemist? We gave summons an hour past. I have a special task that needs his genius. A very special ring born of the bones of a young enchantress…"

"Lord Winter," Didion interrupted, "the alchemist is gone from his hovel."

"Gone?" Morton Winter's eyes narrowed, and he scrutinized closely the captives. "Know any of you this man, the Alchemist?"

No one of the bound party moved or blinked.

Bells jangled from the dais. The fool, near the silver throne, offered, "Perhaps the lunatic blew himself up at last!"

"Shut-up, Fool!"

The bells stilled. Winter turned whitely again to Yda. "You child? Do you know aught?" his cold voice wheedled.

Yda stood mute.

"We'll have more out of you tomorrow. Mark my words, child." Morton Winter menaced spittle and himself hooded Yda anew. "And you other thieving vermin, too!"

The pallid tyrant heaved angrily towards his glittering throne and dropped undecorously down. A fat hand reached for a sweetmeat.

"Didion! Give order that the city gates stay locked come morning. We'll fence the witch in. Mayhaps a fleeing alchemist, too. Ingamald, methinks, will not desert these masqueraders. And set you guards in the alchemist's hilltop home. Blood contract or no for anonymity, we will see the man before our person."

Winter further barked, "And the concealed dungeon door revealed to us by Tabula. Have its secrets been further unlocked? Do we yet know the passage it protects?"

"No, m'lord. Not yet. Sentries are posted thence. A mason works to discover its mysteries."

"Let me assure you, Didion," Winter's voice crackled coldly, "that I hold you personally responsible for unlocking that door. See that it opens!"

"Yes, my lord."

"Now get out! All of you! Take these scum back to the dungeons. Lock them in separate cells. See to it that they are close-guarded round the clock."

"As you will it, Master." Didion bowed and motioned to the guards.

Chains rattled. Feet shuffled. The door clicked securely shut. And Winter, alone, strode over to Tabula.

"Show me the witch, my darling stone siren. Show me. Show me, Tabula."

The black sibyl replied only with a quick image across her face: the flick of an orange tabby's tail. Then she went blank.

Morton moved away from her. In irritation, he poured himself a generous cup of clear distilled liquor. Bottle and goblet in hand, he eased his fat frame into the soft trapezoidal bed. He drained a cup. Another. And another. Gradually, his mood eased. Reassured of his imminent success, he reclined, sipping and smiling.

"Morrrrrrrton, she will come," the first voice breezed.

"Oh, yesssssssss, Morton. Oh, yesssssssss!" The second hissed agreeably.

"The witch. Morton, on the morrow, you will have the witch, Ingamald!" The third caressed his ear.

"A toast to that! Indeed. Indeed." Morton Winter drained a final goblet and threw it gleefully at the dying embers in the fireplace.

"Goodnight, Morton," sighed his left slipper, tossed under the bed.

"Goodnight, Winter," chimed the right, upturned on the white fur bedside rug.

"Indeed. Indeed." His bloodless face relaxed into chilly dreaming.

Ingamald paused at the spell she was re-reading. A massive book lay open before her on the alchemist's great table. The witch could no longer concentrate. Bells had tolled five hours. That was already some time ago. It grew very late.

As the hours crept along, her wiccan options grew fewer: *To be caught as beast at dawn is to never again know human form.* To play the cat was to risk staying the cat.

She was growing frantic. With witch-will, she tried to find her friends: Yda, Lira, Ingo, Erabesque. The Troubadour. But only in her imagination could she conjure their images.

Stomach churning with apprehension, Ingamald strode over to the trap door and threw it ajar, peering into its dark maw. She crept down the ladder and carefully closed the door overhead. With a quick spell murmur, a carpet moved to camoflauge the trapdoor above in the alchemist's workroom.

Glimmering softly in the pitch darkness, the friendly fosfor pebbles led the way. Yda had left a sure trail.

Tripping along the narrow and weeping way, Ingamald, heart in throat, wended the secret passage. Her father's too-long cloak hampered the going. Breathless and harried, she reached the wall. Her witch fingers sought the seventh stone. She touched it and gasped. Hot! Ingamald tried again, pulling her hand back from the heat.

"Something is surely amiss!" she told herself. There was nothing to do but return. Wretched, she backed from the door. Turning, she retraced her steps along the glowing path of pebbles. They stopped just at the foot of the ladder. The witch hastened up the first two rungs, then stiffened.

Voices above, within the alchemist's cottage!

She could neither go forwards nor backwards but stood, frozen, clutching the ladder.

"Leave us, guard!" Didion sharpened his bird's wing voice.

"But I have express orders…"

"From me, the orders came from me, simpleton. Look at her," the misshapen minister pointed to Lira squatting on a filthy mat in her cell, "can this wench overcome a hunchback?"

Grumbling, the guard left them. Didion ungagged the Learned woman. Shamefaced, he sat before her on a three-legged stool.

Lira rubbed the tender skin where the rough rag had bound her mouth. "Thank you, Didion."

"There is little enough to thank me for."

"We're in a pretty predicament, that's certain. But you are not to blame."

"He found you out…through that blasted stone. The Tabula. Morton Winter knew that when your group did not make a move, the tag end of Carnival celebrations would be cue. And so he pleaded with the stone to give up your whereabouts.

"At last, after repeated requests, she complied. She showed him. And he watched you wander the Carnival crowds, saw through your disguises. Had extra sentries posted everywhere. Still you evaded them. And then the Tabula showed him the wall, the secret doorway. She did not show him all. But enough. Armed guards were made ready."

"But the stone did not show him Ingamald?"

"No. And it drives him mad. In desperation will he lure her hither. Tomorrow your public trials… and tortures… will be the bait. All the cells will be emptied. All those he finds guilty will be victim of the Carnival executions. The ignorant masses love bloodsport, and they will be crying out for it."

Didion's hunched back, hunched even further. "You will die, Lira."

"While Ingamald is free, there is hope!"

He turned his pathetic face towards her. "I could help you. But you alone, Lira. I cannot possibly free your friends and be undetected. Tonight, I have a plan…"

"No, Didion. I will not turn coward and desert my friends. Fate has brought me hither for some purpose. Let us see it out."

"Lira…"

"No. But my thanks for your offer."

Sighing, the hunchback stood to go. "Tomorrow you will have a final audience with Morton Winter. If you were to confess—though I know you will not—it would go easier for you."

"You are right. I am no tongue-wag. Besides, Didion." Lira smiled at him. "Whatever have I to confess, having done nothing wrong?"

"'Tis true. You are guilty of no offense. You are merely a Learned. A good woman who reads and shares reading with others."

"It is a gift she gave me, your mother. This vocation. This calling."

"Aye. And me as well." He shuffled to the barred door and unlocked it with his great key.

"Goodnight, friend Didion."

The hunchback could say nothing and so locked the cell door.

Ingamald's hands on the ladder cramped. Suspended thus, she had slowed her pounding heart and managed to think. Three-quarters of an hour at least had crawled by. Dawn was surely approaching. There was little time left for this plan. But mayhaps just enough. And this was the only plan that Ingamald, cold and fatigued, could conceive.

With a soft thud, the alchemist's velvet robe dropped to the damp floor below. Cautiously, the witch climbed the remaining three ladder rungs. Pushing gently on the trapdoor, she eased it open a crack. From beneath the carpet she espied firelight glow. She held her breath, listening.

Snores from the sleeping guards. A creaking chair. No other sound. The witch dared to open the trapdoor further. The hinge, at least, was well oiled. Still no one moved or spoke. She raised the door up and gently lowered it to the floor, creeping up and out quietly on all fours. Then in a whisker's flick, witch turned cat.

Slink, slink, slink past the first guard towards the door. Press of paw and nose to ease it open. Closed and locked. Cat-frustrate! What to do? What to do?

Four men. Four sharp weapons at their sleeping sides.

Through the window cat spies a lightening sky.

What to do?

"Meeeeeeroowwllll. Meeeeerowwllll."

"Eh, what?" grumbles a ruffian.

"Damn cat!" coughs another.

"Meerow. Meerow. Meerow."

"Ah. Poor puss at the door. Needs to go out, does ye? Awright, then." The first rises from his chair. Unwary, unlatches the door.

Cat springs out. Sprints downhill. Towards holly bush. Quickly. Cat-quickly. Before the first dawnlight touches the crest of the hill. No backwards catglance. Dives under spiky cover.

In moments Ingamald emerged becloaked, just as the first ray of dawn touched her face.

A bitter wind swept through her clothing. Where could she hide to stay warm and try to recover her wits? Not Ingo's. That haven was certainly lost. She walked, headbent, down a narrow street. Ahead, a haywagon parked before an inn. Ingamald parted the straw and dug her way within. She covered herself, leaving a small passage for air and light.

Slowly, the warmth crept back into her hands and feet. She breathed deeply.

Horse hooves clopped close to the wagon. Sounds of hitching stirred her from near-slumber. The witch considered how to make escape.

"Yo! Preggett! Man, where ye off to, then?" a male voice cried out from farther down the street.

"I'm off home," a gruff retort sounded from the man hitching the horse to the hay wagon. "I've 'ad enow o' this blasted carny. I want me 'ome and me pipe."

"Nay, man. Ye'll not be a-going anywheres today."

"What?"

"The gates, Preggett. The gates. They're closed, man. Locked up tighter than a woman's will. No one allowed in or out the livelong day."

"Locked, ye say?"

"Aye. By direct order of the Morton Winter, hisself."

"Blasted!"

"Well, there's nought to do fer it, Preggett. Except hie us back to th' pub and start the pints a-flowin'."

"Guess so. I'll take Dez here back to stable then, and meet you at the Pig 'n' Whistle."

"Aye, ye do that then, Preggett."

Sighing in relief, Ingamald listened to the retreating hooves of the horse. Muttering a quickspell of protection, the witch allowed herself to sink deeper into the straw. She tried not to worry about her friends for the moment, certain that they were locked in Winter's dungeon cells, by now. Drained and weary, the witch needed a few hours of sleep before her next course of action. Puzzling over the Bookewoman's riddle, she drifted briefly asleep.

Awaking a few hours later, refreshed, Ingamald knew what she must do. She pulled herself from her straw resting place into the full glare of a winter's morning. Merchants and waresellers were busy at their trades. The witch watched a fisherwoman walk by with basket atop her head. Seconds later, she followed the woman as her twin.

Thus by a series of quick wiccan illusions—knifegrinder, beggar man, apothecary, washing woman—Ingamald made her way unnoticed through the Sprïggen streets towards Winter's castle. She passed through the great gate disguised as chimney sweep. Over the drawbridge as baker. And at the castle doors, she appeared briefly as sentry and so gained entrance unheeded. Within the castle walls she turned liveried servant. Joining the countless other doting and mindless waiting women, she twisted her way through halls and rooms, gradually working her way upwards. Tray in hand, at last she turned the corner to the now familiar upper corridor. Finally, Ingamald, dressed in blue and silver and with powdered wig, put a gloved hand upon the handle of the tyrant's door.

CHAPTER

MORTON WINTER REVELED in his ablutions and sybaritic pleasures most of the morning. He dallied in a tub of suds. Took delight in the trimming of his toenails, the filing of foot callouses. Chose his costume with care. Even entertained an early visit from his fool.

His vastness reclined on the great throne, waited upon by a gloved and powdered servant, when Didion entered with news. The hunchback carried a black velvet cloak.

"Lord Winter," he began, "this is all that remains of the alchemist. It was discovered in a secret passage beneath his hovel. A passage that leads to the mysterious stone wall."

"Bring the garment to me."

Didion crossed the floor, mounted the dais and relinquished the robe. Morton inspected it closely, discovering a pair of spectacles in a pocket.

"Seems he vanished into thin air," the fool jangled. "Something you might like to try someday."

"Silence, you jacksauce!" Morton Winter dropped the spectacles to the cold marble floor of the dais. The right lens cracked. "No matter, Didion. Have the alert put out for the fly-by-night, just in case. In the meantime," Winter continued, "we have more pressing matters." And very deliberately, Winter crushed the specs with his silver slippered foot, grinding the glass under his heel.

"Yes, Master. But there is other news."

Morton Winter raised a white eyebrow.

"The two captives in the tower keep are gone. Stolen in the night."

"Cursed be that witch Ingahag!" Morton Winter spat his disgust into the spittoon to his right.

"Most probably while we were occupied by the dungeon ambush, she freed the two in the tower."

"Why weren't the towers more close guarded?"

"You yourself gave order that extra sentries instead file through Sprïggen streets, stand wait along the city walls, poise weapons at the secret door of the dungeons."

Winter threw the cloak back to Didion. "Burn this! And summon the prisoners! This day will see me route out a witch and burn to cinders her and any who oppose me!"

In short order, the shackled prisoners were led into the cold room by downcast Dagnott. Bedraggled, they slumped together before Morton Winter, still attended by the single servant.

"In your final chance for mercy," his voice dripped icicles, "I demand that you tell me: where is the witch Ingamald?" Winter paused. "Any one of you?"

The Troubadour nodded; a guard removed his gag. "She is fast away from your craven clutch, Lord Coldloins!"

"Ah, the gold-toothed one speaks." Morton Winter leaned forward in his seat. "See to it that the tooth is extracted prior to execution. Dagnott will fashion me a medallion from such a prize."

"Duly noted." Didion scribbled in his notebook.

"Unstop the mouth of the fire-eater." Winter accepted the tray of pastries set before him by the gloved servant.

The guard re-gagged the Troubadour and freed Ingo's mouth.

"Ye'll get nothin' from me, ye frosted flake. Ingamald's fast out o' this miserable palace, that's sure."

"You have heretofore performed within these city walls, have you not?" Winter queried mildly. "Acrobat? Tumbler? Fire-worker?"

Ingo nodded thrice.

"Henceforth, shall we stay your acrobatic antics! Drop him from the strap until his joints dislocate."

"As you will it, Lord Winter." Didion's pen scratched furiously.

Ingo's outcry was muffled by the gag. The white gaze fell upon Erabesque. "And who is this fetching creature? Bring her hither. A dancing girl? Perchance she knows the witch, or if not," Morton licked his blue lips, "perchance she will dance for me tonight…"

The guard removed the rag binding Erabesque's mouth. Once freed, the Musica woman pursed her lips and catapulted a globule of phlegm directly onto Morton Winter's plump, pale cheek.

A horrified servant leapt to the dais to wipe away the spittle and clean the cheek of the blanched lord who shook with fury. "Insolent slattern! Find you nothing to dance for this eve? Then may you never dance again. Didion! Heat up the metal boots for this spitting hussy. Burn her soles to set her begging!"

Didion recorded and Erabesque was gagged anew.

"And you, Learned wench? What have you to say?"

Defiant, Lira shook her head.

"So now, we find your telling tongue is silent. Be it ever so. The scold's bridle will do nicely, Didion, to spike that tongue from tattling and those eyes from peering into books ever again."

Didion's hand shook.

"And finally, the child." At his nod, Yda's eyes and mouth were freed. "Anything to tell us this morn, my pet?"

"Yda is no one's pet, she. And Yda's mouth is firmly set, see?"

"Is it? Well then." Morton turned on Yda a hoarfrost smile. "We'll not kill the innocent. Not with such a power as yours. We first saw fit to have those nimble fingers spin straw to gold…so the legends spoke of you. But I prefer your power to bend and shape.

We've no need of extra fingers, nor have you. Didion!" Winter barked, "Have the swordsman remove the sixth finger of each hand!"

Didion broke the nib of his quill and had to re-cut it.

As he did, the fool, sitting glumly nearby, chose to speak. "Well, aren't we in an inventive mood this merry morn, the last of Carnival."

"It's a merry morn, indeed, fool! The last of this tiresome masquerade. And within the hour we'll have a merry blaze. Dagnott, make fast the device for their viewing. I want these to see it. And the witch will have the privilege of watching her friends suffer, then die. Purge the prisons. We'll burn them all. The people lust for roasted flesh. And fool, hunchback, dwarf, guards, executioner—we will, all of us, be present for the viewing pleasure."

"There is little pleasure in raising a stink!"

"Be still, fool! Or your bells will also meet the swordsman's steel edge and I myself will this day set your arse a-flaming! Now guards! Take these foul malefactors from my sight."

The Troubadour, in his chains, rattled his contempt.

A sudden shift of air, warm and softly scented, wafted through the room. Heads turned in all directions.

"Wait, Winter!" A woman's voice echoed. All motion ceased. "Let them go…" the command continued, "and have me."

"And who, precisely, are you?" Morton Winter demanded of the air.

"I am she who woke a dying prince with a kiss. She who flies by broom. She who thieves your treasures in the night. She who devoured her mother. She with nine lives. And she who can kill or spare Morton Winter."

"Ingamald!"

"Aye!"

"You wish a pact then?"

"A pact. Free these. And take me."

"Done!" Winter commanded, "Show yourself, Ingamald."

So summoned, the liveried servant shimmered into a witch at the left side of the sparkling throne.

A collective gasp circled through the room. Even Morton Winter, fatly in his throne, started.

"Seize her!" Immediately, a threesome of brawny men grabbed Ingamald. She put up no resistance. Her bound companions watched, helpless and fearful. One man tore her cloak away. Another searched her roughly. The third seized the ring on her left hand and passed it to Winter who turned it over admiringly.

He placed the ring on his pinky finger, then padded heavily towards her and took a handful of her flaming hair. With a sudden yank, he wrenched a clump from her head.

Ingamald cried out, clutching her scalp. Chains of the prisoners clanked in alarm.

"Foolish witch! Falling prey to false promises. I have waited long for you."

"I trust I will not disappoint, Morton Winter." Ingamald's green eyes watered, but she did not avert her gaze. Shivering, Winter thrust away her torn tresses.

"Take her! Shear her! Look for the witch's mark. Show no mercy. I will have vengeance, at last." He stormed back to his throne. "Take them all. And within the hour, bring these and the other dungeon scum to the scaffold in the public gardens!"

CHAPTER

I, INGAMALD, AM AFRAID.

They have shorn my hair. It lies in pieces around my feet. They have poked my body. Examined me. Humiliated me. I am dressed in filthy rags. In my terror, I have soiled myself. And where are my friends? This place, these dungeon cells, seem eerily empty.

I do not know if my plan will work. Mayhaps I should have killed the tyrant in the night as I planned.

I wonder if the prophecies at my birth spoke true. Presaging my great power. I do not feel powerful. I do not feel a petty charmer, much less a sorceror. I must not let Morton Winter suspect my fear.

They come. The ones with keys and brute strength. The ones who prodded me. I abhor them. I wish them ill will.

But to feel thus is to succumb. I will numb myself to their rough treatment, their curses. I will still be Ingamald!

They push me forward to the dungeon exit. We march up countless steps, those same I traversed as cat. Weary, I stumble. One man heaves me onward. Finally, the ascent. I am thrust into the cold stark day. Ahead a tumbrel. They tie my neck, my arms and legs to the sides of the cart. I am reminded of my journey as captive to Ruheplatz. The bitter wind whips through my rags. I wonder where my green cloak is and think of Hana. Tears well and I fight to staunch them.

We roll through the swollen streets of a city maddened by Carnival. The citizens scream their insults, and I block my ears. It is not very far to the public gardens from the castle. But by the time we stop, I am numb with cold. Good then. To be numb in such a state is good.

Before me are the other prisoners shackled together, awaiting an incendiary fate. Already the fires at the stakes smoke and smoulder.

On the public scaffold, there are they, my friends. Next to them, reclining on a glittering silver litter, his hideous highness, swollen in sloth and gluttony, covered in ermine robes. The guard propels me closer, the better to see.

Morton Winter drinks freely from a silver flask. He examines his rings. The dragon ring, on his pinky. Will he prick himself and so free us all? Nay, he merely admires the design, strokes the false moonstone.

And even if I can save them from death, can I also spare my friends their tortures?

Before Erabesque, the metal boots over a fire are heating to red, soon to white heat. They will force her feet therein to burn and maim my sister. As Winter promised, ne'er more will those Musica feet dance.

Ingo lies suspended upsidedown with ties to each limb. A hanging man, just as in the Fortuna. At a signal, he will drop and arms and legs will be pulled from their joints. So crippled, he will neither caper nor cavort again.

There is Lira, the scold's cage already fastened to the back of her head, the freakish spiked mask at the ready to be closed. When the hooded executioner slams the cage shut upon her face, it will bore into her eyes and tongue, a terrible fate. A terrible pain.

With fingers splayed atop a chopping block, covered Yda sits trembling. Sharp cleaver poised in butcherous hands, the swordsman only awaits the word to sever each sixth finger from its hand.

And finally, the Troubadour, bound in a chair. Rogues prepare to pry his mouth open. Morton Winter selects the forceps by which he himself will remove the beautiful gold tooth.

So what good am I, a witch bound and trussed? I wince at their impending peril. Their certain pain. But what do I do?

I puzzle over an old woman's riddle thinking therein lies my answer. Go over the spells I read the night previous for some hope. But I am far from hope. And I am sick at heart for these, my beloved friends.

The dread device is wheeled onto the platform. Its huge frame is shrouded in silver silk. Dagnott the dwarf drags me upon the scaffold aside him and the cloaked device. We face the cabal, left of my friends awaiting their torture.

Now we are all together again. We band of rebels. We the notorious, will suffer together. The witch, in watching, perhaps most of all.

Several servants help the luxurious lord from his litter. Nearby the fool fumbles a lame macabre joke. Something about us all being grave men and women. Other than that, my father does nothing but shift from foot to foot. What more can he do? What more would he?

Didion, the hunchback, begins to recite a list of our crimes: treason, kidnapping, plots to murder, and so forth. He drones on as Morton Winter draws nigh.

"Without your hair, witch, methinks you are nothing. Therein, I suspect, lay your power. And now it is gone, with your tresses."

I say nothing, not trusting my voice. I watch him adjust his many rings. On his forefinger is a striking crystal gem. It catches my eye in the winter sunlight, blinding me momentarily.

"Ah, you admire this stone, then? Well, you should. For it was born of the ashes of Hana of Hören Wood."

"What?" I speak without caution.

"Yes. My design. A little alchemy. And Dagnott's shaping."

I swallow my nausea.

"Do you not wish to kill me now, witch? You would, if but you could."

"I had my chance and did not, Morton Winter."

"Eh?"

"I stole into your chamber, up to your very bedside. I looked into your sickly face, and chose to spare your life."

"If such is true, then you are a fool's daughter."

I smile at him. My nausea is passing.

"Wherefore did you not take my life if such was your opportunity?"

I think carefully on my answer. Didion is now reading our sentences; the crowd roars in pleasure at our certain deaths. A sour tomato sails past my left ear. "I choose not to kill. I choose another path. I know there is another way."

"Idiot woman! I mistook you for a wise one, when indeed you are a halfwit. Let me assure you, Ingamald," he wheezes close to my ear, "there will be no negotiations. My will be done!"

Morton Winter strides over to the wild spectators. "Citizens, this day, the last of Carnival, we have a visual spectacle for you! Witness these special treatments chosen especially for these prisoners. You have heard tell of their heinous deeds. Now you will bear witness to their tortures and deaths."

He prattles on, raising his fat arms dramatically, showing off his oratory prowess and his numerous rings. I see again the dragon ring. Hana's gem winks at me in the winter glare.

"Dagnott!" Winter commands.

The dwarf groans, directly behind me.

"Show the worthy Sprïggen citizens what final delight awaits them and these doomed reprobates. Unveil the device!"

Taking hold of the silver wrapping, Dagnott strips the huge structure. The crowd is awed. My friends visibly start. I, too, am dumbstruck by the fiend's imagination for torture.

Before me is the largest looking glass I have ever seen. The snow's reflection in its silver face is so bright, I can scarce look. Housed in an ornate silver frame of gargoyles, imps and hobgoblins who clutch the glass in claw and talon, it is at once hideous and irresistible. I cannot bear to look. I cannot look away.

"Thus will the criminals witness their own agony. A most befitting cadence to the tortures I've selected." Morton Winter swells with pride and can not refrain from admiring himself in the device.

After adjusting his filmy hair, he leans to me again. "I dare you now to do me harm, witch!"

And every impulse in my body urges me to comply.

"Coward!" His spittle is venom to me.

I force my gaze steady. "Look at me, Morton Winter. See before you a coward? No. Neither am I a death-dealer. Yours is the certain road to corruption. Putrescence of the spirit. Look at you, Morton Winter. And see for yourself if my words are false."

He cannot resist a glimpse of himself in his cursed mirror. For a heartbeat, a shadow crosses his pallid face. Snarling, he looks back to me.

"I will enjoy watching the flesh melt from your bones, Ingawitch! I will stay until your final cinder."

I shut my eyes and avert my face from the reek of his breath.

When I look again, the pale one has gone to the front of the platform. More pontificating. Self-aggrandizing. The crowd roars its approval. Hisses at the culprits on the scaffold. Hurls slurs and foul food.

I look at the glass before me. In it, I am bald and beyond ugly. There is a cut along my pate from the rusty razor. Blood dries along the side of my face. I am fascinated.

I see Dagnott's sorry gaze in the mirror beside mine.

"Wenceslas lives," I speak mild and quiet.

Dagnott jerks his gaze to mine in the glass. We look at each other in reverse.

"He has your bright eyes, Dagnott, and no doubt his two dimples match those hidden beneath your yellow beard."

"Where is my son?" the dwarf whispers hoarsely.

"He was kept in the Sprïggen castle tower all this time. Your child stolen by Winter himself. Yestereve, I freed him. Now he is with the princess Gretchen, also liberated. They are safe away from Sprïggen."

Dagnott swallows. "You lie, witch!"

"Why would I?"

"You think to save your life. You think Dagnott will help."

"I need only a diversion, Dagnott."

The dwarf looks away.

"Dagnott. I promise you. Wenceslas lives. Help me."

CHAPTER

FROM SOMEWHERE NEAR THE STAGE, a drum roll sounded. Morton Winter raised his hand, eager to give signal to begin the tortures.

Chuckling coolly, he glanced over his shoulder at Ingamald, daring her to do him injury. His jowls bounced fleshily.

At that precise moment several things happened:

The dwarf roared.

And the fool at Winter's foot cried, "Not even a fool can bear it!" Whereupon he leapt into the crowd and was borne away over the tide of onlookers, a gull riding a wave.

And the hunchback dropped his scroll, raised himself to his fullest possible height and moved to grasp tightly the raised fist of his master.

As Didion struggled to stop the tyrant's signal, Dagnott hurled himself towards the two men in unfettered dwarfish fury.

Ingamald watched agape. And saw.

Morton Winter locked in battle, his fist thrust upwards defiantly. The ring that was Hana sparkling in the tempest, flashing brilliant.

The witch looked back to the glinting reflective glass. In that same instant, she knew.

And Ingamald, at last, looked through the glass and saw.

She spoke soft, at first, then growing to crescendo:

"Let all lie still
Cold and frozen be
But for the twelve-fingered girl
And me!"

The tumult hushed like new falling snow. Next the air chilled until crackling.

Three grappling forms solidified: Winter's corpulence holding erect a blue-white hand, Didion's hunched form in fierce clutch, Dagnott's massive smith's fist poised for a blow. All frozen mid-struggle. A rime grimace upon Winter's face. The talon points of the dragon ring frost-crusted, also the gem that was Hana.

Captive friends on the platform stilled by the cold, looks of shock fast on their faces.

Throughout the crowd, frozen expressions of mockery, surprise, hatred. Hands and arms raised, vegetables set to hurl. Mouths gaped mid-insult or curse.

In the background, fires licked frozen tongues at the stakes. Before them, ice sculptures of the other prisoners.

All was very still as a glacial cold crept throughout the city, around its walls, and beyond. Within mere moments, Hinterlünd succumbed to a frigid sleep. The witch shivered.

A small voice queried, "Ingamald? Where is the 'she'? Yda is so afraid."

"Yda, Ingamald is here." The witch uttered an unbinding spell. Her ropes fell limp to the frosted ground. She made her way to the girl and set her free, finally lifting the hood from the small head.

Yda gasped when she beheld the wiccan woman, bald and bloodied.

"The wicked 'he' has hurt Ingamald!"

"Nay, Yda. I am merely shorn of my locks. They will grow again in time. And the cut is but flesh deep, appearing worse than it truly is."

"What has happened to the Winter?" The child looked about her in wonder. "Everyall has become winter! Are these everyones dead?"

"Are the trees and growing things dead come the snow and icy season, child?"

"Nay. They merely sleeping be."

"And so it is with these, both friend and foe, Yda."

"Are these to sleepy on forever and a day then, Ingamald? Our friends frozen and lost to us? Hinterlünd forever winterland?"

"No one is lost, Yda. All will rouse once more. I will wake them and Hinterlünd again."

"But the cold-blooded lord, too?"

"Aye, even he."

"Then what? We will all be where we began."

"Nay, Yda. Look, you and I are free. Much is different than a few breaths ago."

Incredulous, the child with fingers six and six looked about her. "But how will you free Erabesque and Ingo and Lira and the Troubadour? How will you stop the terrible hand of Winter?"

"An answer to this problem lies elsewhere, Yda."

"Where then, Ingamald?"

"Why, child, through here…"

Taking six fingers of the girls' left hand firmly in her own, the witch pulled her towards Winter's foreboding device.

"Look through, Yda. See what you can see."

Puzzled, the child peered at the glass. "I see Yda. I see Ingamald."

"Nay. Try again. Look *through* the glass."

She squinted and craned her neck, and then, "Oh, Ingamald. What wonders!"

And together, Ingamald and Yda stepped through the glass and beyond.

EPILOGUE

Four feet disappear
through a solid pane of glass
while leagues away in a forest clearing
an old woman locked in hoarfrost
open book upon her knee
sits laughing at some humour
and near the ice castle
of a frost-stilled lord
a frozen fool dances on the hill.

ABOUT THE AUTHOR

Photo by: Geoff McMaster

GAIL SIDONIE SOBAT is a writer and educator at the University of Alberta. She has a Masters in Children's Literature and is the founder of the Youth Write summer camp for young writers. She has also published a book of poetry, *aortic caprice*, and the young adult novel *Ingamald*. *A Winter's Tale* is her second YA novel.

Free Book Club Guides for *A Winter's Tale* are available online at **www.greatplains.mb.ca**.